ALEX KNIGHT
—— AND ——
THE SECRET
WORLDS

ANDROR M. THOMPSON

Copyright © 2023 by Andror M. Thompson

All rights reserved. No part of this book may be reproduced, stored in a retrieval system, or transmitted in any form or by any means, electronic, mechanical, photocopying, recording, or otherwise, without the prior written permission of the copyright owner.

This is a work of fiction. Names, characters, places, and incidents are the product of the author's imagination or are used fictitiously. Any resemblance to actual events, locales, or persons, living or dead, is entirely coincidental.

ISBN: 979-8-86228-345-7
First Edition: 2023

Dedicated to my beautiful wife and to those who inspire and encourage

CONTENTS

CHAPTER ONE 07
a clash of theories and fists
CHAPTER TWO 25
journey into esmeira: unveiling the imagination"
CHAPTER THREE 47
the guide to worlds
CHAPTER FOUR 91
laughter's echo in ludicrous legumes"
CHAPTER FIVE 107
"flight among the avian society"
CHAPTER SIX 123
dimensions united
CHAPTER SEVEN 137
bound by unity: heroes arise
CHAPTER EIGHT 155
"bonds of adventure: a tale of friendship and choices"
CHAPTER NINE 189
the veil of shadows
CHAPTER TEN 197
"dimensional convergence: defending against darkness"
CHAPTER ELEVEN 209
"unleashed shadows: city in chaos"
CHAPTER TWELVE 217
return of the sceptre
CHAPTER THIRTEEN 223
"resilient hearts: a journey of redemption and transformation"
CHAPTER FOURTEEN 237
"the prank portal: unveiling unity, creativity, and laughter"

PROLOGUE

Darkness was his ally as he moved silently under the cover of the trees in the dense forest. His sharp hearing detected their rushing footfalls. His pursuers were going the wrong way. Ruok smiled to himself, he had given them the slip. Looking ahead, he spotted the shimmer of pale moonlight on water. He moved on silently, eager for a drink. The lake was small, its calm placid waters very inviting.

Pushing back his hood, Ruok looked at his reflection. His yellow eyes looked tired from lack of sleep and the hair on his face was dirtied. He cupped some water in his large hands and washed his haggard face. The cool refreshing water relaxed him and he drank deeply. Satisfied and refreshed, he looked up at the far end of the lake. He saw a cave there, partially hidden by rocks. He wondered why the cave's entrance was blocked by rocks placed there on purpose. Then he remembered the strange stories he had heard as a child about a cave that was a portal to other dimensions. Could this be that cave, Ruok wondered?

"There he is." Someone shouted from behind him. "There, by that lake."

"Curses." Ruok whispered.

The Dictator's men had found him. There was no time to lose. The sound of their horses galloping got nearer quite rapidly. Ruok had no other option other than to dive into the lake and swim to the other side. Swimming faster than he had ever done before, Ruok reached the other side and climbed out of the lake, panting and gasping for air. He looked around for a way to get away hidden from sight, but all he saw was open rocky land with no cover. He glanced at the cave, now just a few feet away from him, and wondered if he should run inside.

Whoosh! An arrow whizzed past his head. Ruok ducked down quickly as two more arrows flew past and hit the rocks near him. He made up his mind, the cave it was. Running in a zig zag to dodge more arrows flying at him, he ducked behind some rocks at the cave entrance. He looked back at his pursuers. Some of the Dictator's men jumped into the lake and swam towards him.

"There's only one thing to do now, old boy." Ruok mumbled to himself and began pulling away at the rocks blocking the cave entrance. "Never mind all those crazy stories about the cave being magical."

"There he is… get him." The first of the Dictator's men to reach his side of the lake shouted.

No more time to think now, Ruok decided and pulled away the last rock before running inside. The darkness in the cave was different from the one outside. It felt like a thick substance, even denser than the water of the lake. He felt like he was trapped within it. Ruok understood then that all the stories were true and this cave was indeed a portal to other dimensions. He closed his eyes and mumbled a prayer, ready for the cave to take him away from there…

CHAPTER ONE

A CLASH OF THEORIES AND FISTS

The sun shone brightly through the windows of the classroom, as Mr Wills; a tall and slender man with a brown hair that adds to his professional appearance, stood at the front of the room, a glint of excitement in his eyes. The students settled into their seats, anticipation in the air.

Today's topic was the Big Bang Theory, and Mr. Wills was eager to see what his class knew.

"Good morning, class," Mr Wills began with his characteristic enthusiasm. "Today, we're going to discuss one of the most fascinating theories in astrophysics: The Big Bang Theory."

Whilst writing the words "Big Bang Theory" on the chalkboard and he turned back to face the students, wearing an expectant smile.

"So, what do you all know about the Big Bang Theory? Anyone want to share their thoughts?" Who can tell me what this theory proposes?"

Hands shot up, and Mr. Wills pointed to a timid boy in the back, Alex sporting a low fade haircut and wearing a light grey jumper that resembled a knight's armor, looked more like a quiet observer than an active participant. Nevertheless, he spoke with a hint of excitement, "Well, the Big Bang Theory suggests that the universe originated from a massive explosion, about 13.8 billion years ago."

Mr. Wills nodded approvingly. "Very good, Alex and has anyone ever thought about the possibility of multiple universes being created by the Big Bang?"

A smirk played on Alex's lips. " Mr. Wills, I have a theory that the Big Bang might have led to the creation of not just one universe, but multiple alternate universes as well."

Laughter rippled through the classroom. Lucas Castillo; a stocky teen with gelled black hair complete with a tiny ponytail, a knack for bullying and one of the low-level members of the fearsome street gang "The Hood" surrounded by his two loyal goons Brian a large beefy boy who barely spoke much but grunted and loved to steal food off the younger kids and Breezy a tall, skinny girl sporting a long braided ponytail and hooped earrings who secretly had a crush on Alex and was jealous of Alex's best friend Scarlette but would act mean to him in front of Lucas. They all scoffed loudly.

("The Hood", It was more than just a gang; it was a sprawling criminal enterprise that thrived on chaos, control, and fear. Its tendrils slithered through every crack and crevice of the urban landscape, ensnaring those who dared to venture too close.)

At first glance, "The Hood" might have seemed like a gathering of disaffected

youth, but beneath its surface, it was a formidable force with high-stakes operations and a network of influence that reached beyond anyone's comprehension. Its members, drawn from all walks of life, were united by a twisted sense of loyalty and a desire for power. Lucas Castillo and his school friends, naive and impressionable, found themselves lured into this dark realm.

The true power of "The Hood" resided in its high-ranking adult members, individuals who operated in the shadows with a ruthless efficiency that was both terrifying and awe-inspiring.

These figures were the architects of the gang's vast criminal empire, manipulating markets, politics, and law enforcement to suit their nefarious purposes. Their reach was expansive, and their influence was felt by anyone who lived within the city's boundaries.

Among these adult members, "The Enforcer" was the embodiment of dread. His mere presence was enough to quell any dissent within the ranks.

His reputation for brutal efficiency and unflinching loyalty to the gang was well-earned. Stories of his actions circulated like urban legends, tales of those who had crossed his path disappearing without a trace. He was the embodiment of violence and control, ensuring that the gang's grip remained unyielding.

And then there was "Mr. Big," the enigmatic puppet master who orchestrated "The Hood's" operations from the shadows. His true identity was a closely guarded secret, and even the most senior members of the gang had never laid eyes on him. He was the mastermind behind the gang's strategic maneuvers, the architect of its malevolent plans. His voice carried weight through intermediaries, his orders executed without question. His absence only seemed to enhance his mystique and power, a faceless figure whose influence was felt everywhere but seen nowhere. As Lucas and his school friends ventured deeper into the world of "The Hood," they came face to face with the stark reality of their situation.

The camaraderie they had initially felt gave way to an all-encompassing dread, as they witnessed acts of violence and manipulation that tore at their moral compasses. They had become pawns in a game far beyond their control, entangled in a web of darkness that seemed impossible to escape.

In the depths of this ominous narrative, "The Hood" emerged as a genuine threat to society, a force that subverted justice, distorted truth, and preyed upon the vulnerable. Its power lay not only in its operations but also in the psychological hold it had over its members.

The chilling presence of "The Enforcer" and the elusive "Mr. Big" elevated the gang's aura of danger and invincibility.

In this tale of crime and redemption, Lucas Castillo and his friends personify the struggle against the suffocating grip of "The Hood." As they navigate treacherous waters, they come to realise that breaking

free from its clutches is not just an act of physical escape but a battle for their very souls. Their journey becomes a symbol of hope against insurmountable odds a beacon that reminds us that even in the darkest of times, the human spirit can shine through, inspiring others to rise against the tide of malevolence and forge a new path toward light.

"Oh! Come on, Alex! Multiple universes? That's just science fiction nonsense!"

Alex's cheeks flushed, but he held his ground. He may be shy, but when it came to his theories, he could be surprisingly assertive.

"Well, Lucas, just because something sounds like science fiction doesn't mean it's impossible. The universe is full of mysteries we're still trying to unravel."

Lucas leaned back, laughing mockingly. "You're hilarious, Alex.

You should do stand-up comedy with your alternate universe nonsense."

This was the spark that ignited a fiery exchange of insults between Alex and Lucas.

The class was thoroughly entertained as Alex unleashed a barrage of witty comebacks that had everyone in stitches. Even one of Alex best friends' Scarlette, a cool and fiery girl with beautiful braided hair who usually exuded an air of seriousness and loved to wear red clothing found herself laughing.

Mr. Wills, however, was far from amused. The more they bickered, the more his patience wore thin.

"That's enough!" he finally shouted, his voice echoing in the classroom. "Alex, Lucas, both of you quiet down this instant!"

The bell rang, mercifully ending the class. As students poured out into the corridor, the buzz of excitement filled the air. Alex and his friends huddled together, reliving the witty banter that had taken place.

Alex's best friend, Marcus, a skinny and tall teen wearing a backwards cap and with a penchant for 90s nostalgia, slapped Alex on the back. "Dude, you roasted Lucas and his gang. That was epic!"

Scarlette, in her signature red jacket, chuckled. "Yeah, even I have to admit that was pretty entertaining, Alex."

Spotting Alex amidst the cheerful crowd, Lucas's eyes narrowed with a wave of simmering anger. He couldn't let Alex's cleverness overshadow his popularity.

Pride and ego colliding, Lucas decided to confront Alex once more, hoping to regain his dominance in front of their peers.

Stomping towards Alex, Lucas's footsteps echoed like an approaching storm.

His cronies followed obediently, their expressions a mix of unease and loyalty.

As the students noticed the tension brewing, hushed whispers spread through the crowd like wildfire.

Drawing close to Alex, Lucas couldn't resist the opportunity to belittle him further.

"Hey, Einstein, still think you're smarter than everyone, huh?" he sneered, a malicious grin tugging at his lips.

Alex, who had hoped the day would end peacefully, bristled at the insult but tried to keep his cool.

"Lucas, let's not do this. The day is over, and there's no need for any more trouble."

But Lucas, drunk on the rush of power, wasn't interested in de-escalation.

He poked Alex's chest with a finger, taunting him, "What's the matter?

Too scared to defend yourself without your little science tricks?"

Scarlette sighed and whispered in Alex's ear "Don't do it Alex, he's not worth it man"

The tension in the corridor heightened, and the surrounding students sensed that things were about to explode.

Unwilling to be pushed around, Alex clenched his fists, his patience wearing thin.

"Ain't got your daddy around anymore?"

Marcus looked at Lucas in shock "Don't have that Alex! You need to teach him a lesson!"

"No he doesn't Marcus! Can't you see that's what Lucas wants?" Scarlette protested.

Alex couldn't hear his friends arguing, all he could see was red.

Lucas friends' snickered and Alex felt a surge of anger rising deep within his heart as if it was lava about to explode from him as if he were a volcano.

Alex's dad had passed away a few years ago due to cancer.

"That's it Lucas. You asked for it," he growled, his voice low and fierce.

The insults and threats escalated, pushing Alex to his breaking point. Before anyone could react, fists were flying. The corridor erupted in cheers as students formed a circle around the brawl.

Amidst the chaos, Mr. Wills came charging through the crowd, his face red with anger. He forcibly separated Alex and Lucas, his voice booming with fury. "That's enough! Both of you, my office, now!"

The two adversaries were led away, their adrenaline-fueled clash earning them a stint in detention. The onlookers slowly dispersed, chattering excitedly about the brawl they had just witnessed.

In the aftermath of the fight, the corridor was left with palpable tension. The camaraderie among the friends remained, but a lingering unease hung in the air.

Detention was a stifling room filled with a mixture of boredom and tension. Alex sat there, fidgeting with his fingers, his mind replaying the fight that had just transpired in the corridor. Beside him sat Lucas, his face a mixture of resentment and anger.

The door creaked open, and in walked Mr. Ransford; a tall athletic man and the stern but fair head teacher of the school.

His presence commanded respect, and the room fell into an uneasy silence as all eyes turned toward him.

"Good afternoon, gentlemen," Mr. Ransford began his voice a mixture of disappointment and authority.

"I had hoped that we wouldn't have to meet under these circumstances, but it seems we find ourselves here."

Alex kept his gaze lowered, his cheeks still flushed with the remnants of his earlier anger.

Lucas, on the other hand, stared defiantly at Mr. Ransford, his posture rigid.

"Alex, Lucas," Mr. Ransford continued, his gaze sternly fixed on each of them in turn, "fighting in the corridors is not only against school rules, but it's also a display of immaturity that reflects poorly on your characters."

Lucas opened his mouth to retort, but Mr. Ransford's raised hand silenced him. "I understand that there might have been differences, but violence is never the solution. It's crucial to find healthier ways to resolve conflicts."

Alex nodded, his guilt weighing heavily on him. He hadn't intended for the situation to escalate the way it did.

Mr Ransford's gaze softened slightly as he turned his attention to Alex. "Alex, I've heard from Mr Wills about your enthusiasm for theories and ideas. That's an admirable trait, but remember, you're capable of using your intellect to handle situations better."

Alex swallowed hard, feeling a mixture of embarrassment and gratitude. "I know, Mr. Ransford. I should have handled things differently."

"Exactly," Mr. Ransford replied. "It's important to not allow others to get under your skin. People will challenge you, but it's up to you to rise above it."

As Mr Ransford continued to talk, his words began to resonate with Alex.

The fight had been a result of his inability to control his emotions, and he needed to learn from this experience.

The head teacher's gaze shifted to Lucas.

"Lucas, your actions are equally unacceptable. Picking fights doesn't make you strong or respected; it only shows a lack of restraint."

Lucas shifted uncomfortably in his seat, his earlier bravado slowly crumbling under Mr Ransford's stern words.

"In any case," Mr. Ransford concluded, his tone firm, "I'll be informing your parents about this incident.

They need to be aware of what's happening at school."

Alex's heart sank. He knew he was going to have to face his step dad's wrath. As the meeting came to an end, he and Lucas were dismissed from detention, leaving them with a heavy sense of responsibility.

As they walked out of the detention room, Lucas shot Alex a begrudging nod. "This isn't over Alex; you better watch your back"

Alex sighed, but it was the thoughts of his mistake weighing on him that concerned him more than Lucas' threats.

Walking out of detention, Alex felt a mix of remorse and determination. He knew he had to work on controlling his emotions and using his intelligence to navigate difficult situations. With Mr Ransford's words echoing in his mind, he was determined to be a better role model for his peers and make his school proud once more.

The school was done for the day; most of everyone had gone home. He walked down the empty hallway with his friends and out of the main gate.

"So what are you going to tell your step dad when he finds out?" Marcus asked concernedly.

"Well Alex should've thought about that before letting that idiot Lucas get under his skin" Scarlette replied

"Look guys, not now. I'm already in enough trouble and don't need to be reminded" snapped Alex

"So that means you won't be able to come over tonight? I got the new Space Blasters video game and Scarlette and I are going to..."

"Marcus!" Scarlette nudged him looking at Alex guiltily.

"Guys I really wish I could come but I'm probably going to be in serious trouble for this. Have fun without me" Alex sighed.

Alex trudged home with a heavy heart, carrying the weight of his actions on his shoulders.

As he opened the front door, he braced himself. He was met with the stern gaze of his stepdad.

Mr. Ransford's words had left an impression on him a reminder that using his brain, thinking before acting, and controlling his emotions were the paths to becoming a better person.

The atmosphere in the house was tense as Alex stepped through the front door. The echoes of his stepdad's stern words still reverberated in his mind. The confrontation in school had been bad enough, but now he had to face his stepdad's wrath at home.

Alex's stepdad Mr. Paul; A tall and burly man with a pointed nose and an imposing presence, was waiting in the living room. His brow was furrowed in anger as he crossed his arms over his chest. "You think you can just go around fighting in school, Alex?

Is that how you're going to make a name for yourself?"

Alex's gaze dropped to the floor, his heart sinking. He knew his stepdad Mr. Paul could be overly harsh, and the thought of another lecture weighed heavily on him.

His mother Joanna Knight; a lady in her late thirties with dark curly hair and a caring face, entered the room. Her expression held a mixture of disappointment and worry. She cast a cautious glance at her husband before turning her attention to Alex.

"Alex, what happened?"

Alex hesitated, his emotions still raw from the fight and the encounter with Mr. Ransford. He knew his mother cared, but he was in no mood to recount the incident. "It's nothing, Mum. Just some stupid fight."

His mother gently touched Alex's arm, her voice softening. "Alex, we're worried about you. We want to make sure you're alright."

But his stepdad wasn't as patient. "Alright? He needs to learn some discipline, not act like a thug in school!"

The tension escalated, with anger. Alex felt trapped in the middle of their conflicting emotions.

Tears welled up in Alex's mother's eyes as she turned to her husband. "Please, let's not make this worse. Yelling won't solve anything."

He grumbled but seemed to relent a little. "Fine, but he needs to know this kind of behavior won't be tolerated."

Alex's room felt like a sanctuary as he stormed away from the argument. He slammed the door behind him, his fists clenched. He threw himself onto his bed, his mind a whirlwind of frustration and resentment.

He wished, not for the first time, that he had a different family situation.

He picked up his favorite novel, a tale of magical worlds and epic adventures. As he flipped through the pages, the words transported him to a place where he could escape from his troubles. He often imagined himself in the shoes of the brave protagonists, fighting dragons and exploring enchanted realms.

He sighed, gazing at the cover of the book. In those stories, he could be someone extraordinary, someone who didn't have to deal with fights, arguments, and school drama. He longed for an escape from the reality that weighed him down.

His thoughts drifted to Lucas, the popular kid who seemed to glide through life effortlessly.

Alex wished he had that kind of confidence and charm. He wished he could be well-liked, respected, and never have to face the sneers of bullies.

With a heavy heart, he set the book aside, his mind still a whirlwind of emotions.

He lay back on his bed, staring at the ceiling, lost in his thoughts. His mind wandered to a world of magic and wonder, a place where he could leave his troubles behind.

As the evening sun cast a warm glow through his window, Alex's room became a cocoon of solace. He yearned for a way to escape not just into the pages of a book, but into a world where he could truly be himself, where his dreams were within reach, and where the challenges he faced were ones he could conquer. In that quiet moment, he closed his eyes, wishing for a different kind of adventure to come his way.

The next day, Saturday morning arrived with a weight of boredom hanging over Alex. He was grounded, a consequence of the fight that had taken place at school. While his parents were out running errands, Alex's thoughts were fixated on the unfairness of his situation.

In his brooding, his phone buzzed with a message from Marcus. "Hey, meet us at the usual spot. Burgers on us!"

The temptation was strong; Alex knew he was grounded but spending the day with his friends seemed like the perfect antidote to his gloomy mood. He checked the clock – his parents wouldn't be back for a while. He could sneak out just for a little while.

With this in mind, Alex slipped out of the house. He met Marcus and Scarlette at their favorite burger joint called Super Burger. Their laughter and camaraderie instantly lifted his spirits.

The aroma of sizzling burgers combined with the carefree atmosphere made Alex momentarily forgot the argument at home and the recent fight at school.

They devoured their Super burgers which was a thinly fried mashed potato and vegetable patty on top of a beef patty giving the benefit of having a beef, potatoes and vegetable meal all wrapped in a bun. Delicious! Alex thought. They sipped on their favorite sweet and savory drinks which were strawberry and ice cream brews and Sweet Potato Juices. The laughter between Alex, Marcus, and Scarlette was infectious. The cosy corner booth they occupied provided the perfect sanctuary for their camaraderie.

Marcus, with his unruly mop of hair and quick wit, playfully jested,

"You know, Alex, if your stepdad found out you're here right now, he'd probably ground you for another century."

Scarlette, her eyes twinkling with mischief, added, "Yeah and I can already hear him saying, 'If you can't follow the rules at home, you shouldn't be hanging around with these troublemakers!'"

Alex rolled his eyes, a smirk forming at the corner of his lips. "Oh, come on, you two. You make it sound like he's the supreme ruler of the universe. Who cares about his rules anyway?"

Marcus raised an eyebrow, taking a sip of his drink. "Well, maybe the fact that he's your stepdad and your mum's kinda scared of him?"

"Scared? Seriously?" Alex scoffed a hint of defiance in his tone. "I can handle myself, guys. Besides, he's not my real dad. I don't see why I should let him dictate every little thing I do."

Scarlette leaned forward, her eyes searching his. "We get it, Alex but you know, we're just worried. We're your friends, and we've seen how things can escalate when you two clash."

Alex's demeanor shifted slightly. He stared at the half-eaten burger on his plate, a mixture of frustration and vulnerability flickering in his eyes. "You think I don't know that? It's just... He's not exactly the easiest person to deal with."

Scarlette softened her tone, reaching across the table to pat Alex's hand. "We're not trying to boss you around, man. Just looking out for you. You're like a brother to us."

"Yeah, Alex," Marcus chimed in. "We're here for you, no matter what but remember, we're not invincible, and trouble seems to have a way of finding us."

Alex let out a sigh, his resistance waning as he met his friends' sincere gazes. "Alright, alright. I hear you. I'll be more careful. Happy now?" Marcus grinned, raising his Strawberry Ice cream brew in a mock salute. "That's the spirit, pal and hey, even if your stepdad is a pain, at least you've got us to make life interesting." He laughed.

Scarlette winked. "And if you ever need a distraction from his lectures, just give us a shout. We'll be your personal escape artists."

Alex couldn't help but chuckle, a genuine smile spreading across his face. "Thanks, guys. I guess I could use a few more escape routes in my life."

(With their laughter carrying through the air, they continued to enjoy their meal, their friendship stronger than ever. Little did they know that

the escapades awaiting them would far surpass any they had encountered before – especially the astonishing discovery that awaited Alex in the depths of the underground tunnel, an adventure that would change everything.)

As they laughed, the three of them got up and stepped out of the burger joint then suddenly he caught a glimpse of a familiar figure out the window – Lucas and his gang approaching. "Oh great" he thought.

"Well, well, look who it is?" A rough voice made them stop dead in their tracks.

It was Lucas, the bully and he loved to make all sorts of trouble for Alex.

"Alex Knight and his two sidekicks." The tall girl standing next to Lucas laughed.

Behind the two of them, a taller and broader boy stood silently, glaring ahead with his black beady eyes.

"Lucas," Alex said with a sheepish grin. "Breezy; a tall girl although is attracted to Alex but she tries to prove strong head and of course, Big Brian; a taller and broader boy with his black beady eye.

"Well, it's nice to see the three of you still sharing the one brain between yourselves." laughed Alex.

Marcus and Scarlette stared open-mouthed at Alex. He was as crazy as he always was with that smart mouth of his. Lucas would not take this insult gracefully.

"So, Knight." Lucas had a cold smile on his thin lips. "You think you're so smart. But you're not, you see. Messing with members of 'The Hood' isn't something smart boys do."

"It should be all right then." Alex grinned back.

"Seeing that The Hood hasn't any smart boys, to begin with."

"You won't be feeling so smart when we smash all your teeth in," Lucas growled and rushed at Alex and they all broke into a run.

Breezy and Brian were right on Lucas's heels. Alex leapt back and spun around. He was off and running as soon as his feet touched the ground. He looked back over his shoulder and stuck his tongue out at the enraged trio of bullies after him, making them even angrier. Alex and his friends split up during the chase,

After losing the gang and hiding in a nearby alleyway, Alex found himself at the entrance of a narrow, dimly lit passage.

The walls seemed to close in around him, and he could hear the footsteps of Lucas and his gang growing fainter behind him... Desperation gave him the courage to plunge into the dark unknown.

As he ventured deeper, the passage opened up into an astonishing sight an abandoned London underground tunnel filled with the unexpected. Abandoned roller coaster tracks snaked through the space, their rusted frames carrying roller coaster trains but these weren't ordinary roller coasters; they were unlike anything he had ever seen. They seemed to shimmer with an otherworldly energy.

Alex's eyes widened as he realised that each roller coaster train was heading toward a different portal, each labelled with a different destination. And one of those portals bore the name "Esmeria." He contemplated heading back outside and looking for his friends until he heard Lucas' voice from a distance which appeared to be sounding nearer and that decided him. "The hell with it" he thought. "My life here sucks anyways" and proceeded to go further into the station

CHAPTER TWO

JOURNEY INTO ESMEIRA: UNVEILING THE IMAGINATION"

Alex stood at the threshold of a mystery, his heart pounding with a mixture of excitement and trepidation.

The portal labelled "Esmeira" beckoned to him like a doorway to another realm, a realm that held the promise of adventure and answers to the questions that had been swirling in his mind.

He hesitated for only a moment before his curiosity and a sense of urgency propelled him forward. With a deep breath, he stepped off the platform onto the roller coaster train and strapped himself in his seat. "Esmeria, here I come!" he said excitedly and the train as if obeying his command, shot off like a bullet with Alex feeling a tingling sensation wash over him as he crossed the threshold of the portal.

In an instant, the world around him transformed. Colours danced and swirled, and he felt as if he was being pulled through a tunnel of shimmering light. He closed his eyes momentarily, his senses overwhelmed by the sensation of movement.

When he opened his eyes again, he found himself in a place that defied description. The air was charged with otherworldly energy, and the landscape was a surreal blend of vibrant colours and unfamiliar structures.

The train then slowed down and stopped at a platform that was suspended in mid-air, overlooking a breath-taking expanse that stretched into the distance. He stepped onto the platform and before him, a sprawling city emerged its architecture was a fusion of futuristic designs and fantastical elements. Towers of glass and metal reached for the sky, adorned with intricate patterns and earn ethereal glow. Bridges arched gracefully between buildings, and colossal sculptures seemed to defy gravity.

Alex's heart raced as he took in the sight before him. He was in Esmeira, a world beyond his wildest imagination. The roller coaster tracks continued from where he stood, weaving through the city like a network of veins, inviting him to explore further.

Everything looked the same in every direction, and the more he looked, the more terrified Alex felt. This has got to be a dream, he told himself again and again. He looked down at his feet and hands. He was there in one piece, still wearing his trainers, jeans, and hoodie. So, where am I? Just as he thought that, the swirling mist parted under his feet, and Alex felt himself falling into the darkness below.

He opened his mouth to scream, but no sound he could hear. He kept falling, lower and lower, until suddenly he stopped, and the darkness gave way to light. He found himself lying on green grass with tall trees overhead, and the sound of laughter and singing was all around him. Alex sat up and stared.

All around him were creatures, some human, some animals, and some that defied his imagination. He shivered slightly, trying to make sense of all of this.

Then a thought lit up in his head. This was a video game. He must be inside a video game. He peered hard at the other creatures around him and the more he looked at them, the more he could recognise that they strongly resembled characters from the video games, movies, cartoons, and comic books that he enjoyed.

This had to be a dream, he told himself again, and he wondered if he would ever wake up from it.

As he cautiously walked through the vibrant realm, Alex's senses were filled with wonder and amazement. Creatures unlike anything he had ever seen frolicked through the verdant landscape.

Among them, he spotted the mischievous Snake Legs a serpentine creature with four gangly legs that moved with uncanny agility. Its bite, though not poisonous, inflicted a brief, intense pain that left victims momentarily frozen, allowing the creature to steal items or food while taunting its prey.

In the gardens of Esmeira, Alex came across the enigmatic Head Fruits.

These peculiar fruits resembled pumpkins, but their faces were those of grumpy old men. Sleeping soundly until disturbed, the moment they were awoken, they bombarded intruders with sarcastic insults. To silence their mockery, one had to pick them up and throw them far away. As they spun through the air and landed in a disoriented daze, their insults gave way to momentary confusion, allowing respite from their verbal barbs.

And then there were the Firework Flies, ethereal creatures that radiated dazzling colours like exploding fireworks.

They floated through the air, leaving trails of vibrant light that painted the skies with their radiant beauty.

As Alex ventured deeper into the realm, he saw in the distance a society of humanoid birds in the enchanted forests. These avian beings, known as the Sylvan wing, lived in an advanced society intricately woven within the woodland. Proud and reclusive, they regarded humans with skepticism, prioritising their own well-being above all else.

In the midst of this breath-taking world, Alex's heart raced with a blend of excitement and trepidation. The creatures that surrounded him were a testament to the boundless imagination that the realm of Esmeira held.

Each encounter promised new surprises, challenges, and opportunities for connection.

"You there, stay where you are."

A loud voice shattered his train of thought.

"You are a trespasser."

"I might be," Alex turned to face the sound of the voice,

"If I knew where exactly I was."

"A smart mouth, eh?" The tall and very broad golem leaned down over him.

"Who, me?" Alex pretended to look surprised. "I'm just Alex, Alex Knight."

"Well, we will see what Her Majesty says about that." The bulky golem replied.

"Her Majesty?" Alex looked hard at the rocky being before him.

"You mean... the Queen is here?"

"Queen Vesta, she is the overseer of the world." The being replied coldly. "Now come, she will know what to do with trespassers like you."

"You'll have to make me, big guy." Alex laughed and began running off in the opposite direction.

And then, to his horror, he found himself turning around and running in step right behind the tall creature into another portal that opened up before him.

The other side of the portal opened into a large palatial throne room full of strange creatures in all sorts of rich finery.

At the centre of the room, seated on a high throne, a young woman of radiant beauty dressed in white and gold looked down at Alex as he followed his captor in through the portal.

"Here he is, Your Eminence." The tall golem bowed before the radiant woman seated on the large throne made of some bright substance.

"This trespasser I found in the Gardens of Aralias."

"Well done, Gurdon." The young queen-like woman nodded at the tall one.

"You may leave now."

Alex's captor bowed and left through the portal.

"Who are you?" Alex wasted no time asking the ethereal woman.

"Where am I? And why?"

"You are Alex Knight." The woman said without emotion.

"Yes, I am." He stared at her in awe. "But how did you...?"

"This is Esmeira, the Vale of Portals." She replied.

"And I am Vesta, the overseer of the world of Esmeira."

"You... are a goddess?"

"I am the overseer and the queen of this world"

"Then you have goddess powers?"

"I do indeed."

"You can send me home?"

"I can, young one," Vesta said. "But you have come here for a purpose.

There has been a breach in the protocol of the portals. Someone has violated our sacred laws... and you have been summoned here to right that breach."

"You mean, I've been brought here to... to be like a hero and save the day." (*Alex eyed the queen suspiciously.*)

"Indeed, you may have, for I am yet to find out where and why the breach has occurred," Vesta said sorrowfully.

"For with each passing moment, the Ancient Sacred Sceptre weakens, and with it, the magic that keeps Esmeira alive."

She spoke of an ancient sceptre, a powerful artefact with a brown and silver decorated handle, crowned by a small purple glowing jewel.

This sceptre had been the guardian of Esmeira for centuries, a beacon of protection against the horrors of the dark dimension, a realm of darkness and chaos that threatened to spill into both Esmeira and Alex's world.

"The sceptre held the power to seal off the terrors of the dark dimension," Vesta explained, her eyes holding a deep sadness.

"Its absence has left Esmeira vulnerable, weakening the barriers that protected us and our world."

Alex listened, his heart heavy with the weight of the revelation. The sceptres theft had set into motion a chain of events that now endangered both realms. He could feel the urgency in Vesta's words, the desperation to convey the gravity of the situation.

"Someone from another dimension," Vesta continued, her voice tinged with concern, "driven by a thirst for power, had stolen the sceptre but also lost it in the process.

They seek its ancient magic, for with it, they could wield the power to control dimensions, to become a ruler of unimaginable might."

Alex's mind raced, connecting the dots of the story. The sceptre wasn't just a relic; it was a key to the very fabric of reality.

Its theft posed a dire threat to Esmeira, his world, and the delicate balance that held everything together.

"Esmeira's magic is waning," Vesta's voice trembled, "and we are open to attacks from the dark dimension. The darkness is seeping through, threatening to consume us."

Alex's determination grew stronger with each word Vesta spoke. He understood the magnitude of the situation and the role he was being called to play.

The ordinary life he had known was now intertwined with a destiny that spanned realms.

"Alex," Vesta's eyes held his with a mixture of hope and solemnity,

"You have been chosen. Chosen to restore the sceptre, to mend the breach, and to protect Esmeira and your world from the impending darkness."

"But why me?" Alex wondered. "I'm just an ordinary kid who doesn't get much respect at school nor at home" Alex said sadly.

"Alex it's often the chosen ones whose hearts possess a uniqueness about them that makes them special and separate from the rest" Vesta replied "Some will give you a hard time because they do not understand you and they are subconsciously threatened by the unique gifts you possess even if you do not realise it. You have been called to greatness" Vesta smiled.

As Vesta's words echoed in the grove, a surge of determination coursed through Alex's veins. He was no longer an ordinary young man; he was a guardian, a defender of realms, tasked with a mission that transcended the boundaries of reality.

In the grove illuminated by the fading sunlight, Alex's gaze locked onto Vesta's eyes, his heart both heavy with the weight of his newfound destiny and alight with a determination he had never experienced before.

He stood at the precipice of a journey that would test his courage, challenge his understanding of reality, and propel him into a world of magic and danger.

Vesta's lips curved into a faint smile, acknowledging the mix of emotions swirling within him. "Alex," she began, her voice carrying soothing warmth, "the Ancient Sacred Sceptre is the key to restoring the balance, to saving Esmeira and your world from the impending darkness."

Alex's eyes narrowed, his focus sharpening.

"But how can I do that? How can I find the sceptre?"

Vesta's gaze seemed to pierce through him as if searching his very soul. "You possess a unique connection, Alex Knight.

A connection to both realms that is rare and powerful. It is this connection that will guide you, that will enable you to traverse the boundaries and uncover the truth."

Alex felt a shiver run down his spine, a mixture of excitement and trepidation. He had never considered himself anything more than an ordinary person, yet now, he was being told that he held a connection to a realm beyond his understanding.

"Close your eyes, Alex," Vesta instructed gently. "Open your mind and reach out with your senses."

With a deep breath, Alex obeyed. He closed his eyes, allowing his mind to open itself to the possibilities that lay beyond the physical world. Almost immediately, he felt a surge of energy, a tingling sensation that seemed to envelop him.

"Feel the currents of magic," Vesta's voice seemed to echo from all around him. "Sense the threads that bind Esmeira and your world together."

Images flashed before Alex's mind's eye vibrant landscapes, swirling colours, and a sense of interconnections that he had never experienced before.

"Now, focus on the sceptre," Vesta's voice was a soothing guide. "Feel its essence, its energy."

As he focused his thoughts, Alex felt a pull, a magnetic force that seemed to beckon him forward. He saw flashes of the sceptre the brown and silver handle, the small purple jewel, and the immense power it held.

"It calls to you, Alex," Vesta's words resonated within him. "It seeks its Guardian, the one who will wield its power for the greater good."

Alex's heart raced as the sensations intensified. He felt as if he were on the cusp of something extraordinary, a destiny he had never imagined.

"The path to the sceptre will not be easy," Vesta's voice grew sombre. "The realm of Esmeira is filled with challenges and mysteries, and the forces that seek to keep the sceptre hidden are formidable but the more worlds you travel to the more you will absorb some of its magic powers..."

Alex nodded, his determination unwavering. He knew that the journey ahead would be fraught with dangers, but he was ready to face them, to fulfil the role that had been thrust upon him.

"Once you find the sceptre," Vesta's voice carried a sense of urgency, "you must restore its magic, mend the breaches between dimensions, and thwart the plans of the inter dimensional thief."

With a final surge of energy, the sensations began to fade, and Alex found himself back in the grove, his eyes meeting Vesta's once more.

"You are the Guardian, Alex Knight," Vesta's gaze held a mixture of pride and hope. "With the sceptre in your hands, you can save Esmeira, protect both realms, and prevent the darkness from consuming all that we hold dear."

Alex's fists clenched, a fire burning within him. He had been given a purpose, a mission that transcended his existence. The sceptre's fate, and the fate of realms, rested upon his shoulders.

Vesta extended her hand toward him, and within it materialised an image an image of the sceptre, its brown and silver handle, and the small purple jewel glowing with an otherworldly light.

"Take this image with you, Alex," Vesta's voice was a whisper carried on the wind. "Let it guide you, let it fuel your determination.

Trust in your connection to both realms and know that you are not alone on this journey."

As the image imprinted itself upon Alex's mind, he felt a surge of energy, a bond forged between him and the sceptre.

The grove seemed to shimmer around him, the boundaries between dimensions blurring for a brief moment.

"Remember," Vesta's voice echoed through the grove, "the destiny you now embrace will lead you to the heart of Esmeira, to the challenges that await, and to the power that will save us all."

And as the last echoes of her words faded, Alex felt a sensation of falling, of being pulled through time and space. He was on the threshold of a new reality, a reality where he would be called upon to stand against the encroaching darkness, to become the Guardian of the sceptre, and to fulfil a destiny that spanned realms.

As the world around him shifted and transformed, Alex braced himself for the unknown, his heart determined, and his mind focused on the task ahead.

(The Chronicles of Esmeira were just beginning, and he was ready to face the challenges, embrace the magic, and forge his own path in a world that defied all understanding.)

"Indeed, Alex Knight, it is good that you understood so quickly," Vesta smiled.

"I will personally guide you about everything that you need to know and then you must return home and wait for the moment you are summoned to play your part. But remember; tell no one of this in your home world. We cannot take the chance of endangering more lives than necessary."

Vesta gave him an ancient golden leather book called "Guide to Worlds" which contains some magical rhymes which will serve as a transporter that will whisk him to different dimensions. "But Your Eminence"; A whiny voice sliced into their conversation.

"Is this wise... to have this, this young child to be bestowed with such great responsibility?"

Alex turned around, and his eyes went wide. "Wow! Is that Super..."

"Do not mind him, Alex Knight." Vesta said indifferently. "That is one of our council members. It is his task to object to everything the council presides upon, just to keep things interesting. It is best to ignore him."

"But why does he look like that?" Alex stared at the tall muscular man in tights.

"Except for the colours of his costume being reversed, he could as well be Super-."

But before Alex could finish, he found himself being sucked into another portal and whisked away down a dark tunnel.

The sensation was disorienting. The tunnel seemed to stretch on forever, and Alex felt a strange mix of fear and exhilaration as he hurtled through the dimensions.

Moments later, the tunnel spat him out into a vibrant and bustling market square. A mix of exotic aromas filled the air, and vendors shouted in a myriad of languages.

Alex stumbled, trying to regain his balance as he marvelled at the bizarre sights and sounds around him.

As he took in his new surroundings, a voice echoed in his mind. "Hey there, rookie! Welcome to the Living App Dimension! I'm your guide, Dippy!"

Alex turned around, searching for the source of the voice, and then he saw it a small, spherical creature hovering in the air before him. It had a mischievous grin and eyes that seemed to be made of pixels.

"Uh, hey there, Dippy." Alex raised an eyebrow. "You're my guide?"

"You got it, buddy!" Dippy zipped around him, leaving a trail of pixilated sparkles.

"I'm here to help you navigate the Living App Dimension, where every app comes to life! And guess what?

You've got apps for super cool stuff like magical spells, gear upgrades, and even snacks!"

Alex blinked in disbelief. This was definitely not part of any video game he'd ever played.

"All right, Dippy." Alex chuckled. "Lead the way."

"Time to get app-happy!" Dippy chirped and zipped ahead, leaving a trail of colourful sparkles for Alex to follow.

As Alex explored the Living App Dimension, he couldn't help but marvel at the endless possibilities.

He encountered fantastical creatures, haggled with animated vendors, and even tried out a few magical spells from his newfound app collection.

With Dippy's fast-talking guidance, Alex was soon navigating the vibrant dimension like a pro.

After what felt like hours of exhilarating exploration, Dippy led Alex to a quaint-looking shop nestled between two towering buildings.

The sign above the entrance read "Dimensional Gadgets & Gears."

"Step right in, Alex!" Dippy exclaimed. "This is the go-to place for all your gear and gadget needs. And trust me, with the quest you're on, you'll need some serious upgrades."

Alex entered the shop, and his eyes widened at the array of fantastical gadgets on display.

From enchanted swords to high-tech goggles, there was something for every type of adventurer.

"Welcome, welcome!" a jovial figure behind the counter greeted Alex.

The shopkeeper was a short, stout creature with a long white beard and twinkling eyes.

"I am Glimwick, the gadget guru. How can I assist you today?"

"Dippy here says I might need some upgrades for the quest I'm on,

" Alex said, trying to wrap his head around the situation.

"Ah, I see!" Glimwick rubbed his hands together. "A quest, you say? Well, you're in luck. I've got just the thing."

For the next hour, Alex browsed through the shop's collection, trying on magical amulets, testing out fantastical boots, and even considering a miniature dragon companion that breathed actual fire.

Dippy provided his energetic commentary, helping Alex understand the benefits of each item.

As Alex was about to leave the shop, his eyes landed on a peculiar item a sleek, futuristic device with glowing buttons and a holographic display.

"That looks pretty useful," Alex mused.

Dippy nodded enthusiastically. "Oh, absolutely! It's like a magical Smartphone for inter-dimensional adventurers! Glimwick says this one's on the house!"

Alex smiled. "All right, I'll take it."

Glimwick's grin widened as he carefully handed over the Dimensional Communicator. "A wise choice, young adventurer. This gadget will serve you well on your quest. And remember, if you ever need more gadgets or upgrades, "Glimwick's the name to remember!"

As Alex left the shop, he felt a newfound sense of determination. Armed with his upgraded gear and Dippy's guidance, he was ready to embrace his role in this bizarre, yet exciting, inter-dimensional adventure.

Little did he know that his journey was just beginning, and the fate of Esmeira and countless dimensions hung in the balance.

With each step, Alex was about to uncover secrets, face formidable challenges, and forge alliances with beings he had only dreamed of encountering before and as he ventured deeper into this extraordinary tale, the lines between reality and fantasy would blur, leading him to discover the true hero within himself.

Days turned into weeks as Alex delved into the heart of Esmeira's mysteries.

Guided by Vesta and aided by Dippy, he navigated treacherous landscapes, battled mythical creatures, and solved intricate puzzles that guarded the path to the Ancient Sacred Sceptre.

Along the way, he met a cast of colourful characters, each with their own unique abilities and stories.

One such character was Lyra, a swift and agile rogue who hailed from a realm of shadows. With her emerald eyes and quick wit, she had a knack for infiltrating enemy camps and gathering vital information.

Despite their initial differences, Alex and Lyra quickly formed a bond of trust and camaraderie.

"You're not like most inter-dimensional visitors," Lyra remarked one evening as they shared stories by the campfire. "You've got this... determination in your eyes."

Alex smiled, gazing into the flickering flames.

"Maybe it's because this adventure feels more real than anything I've ever known."

Lyra's lips curved into a soft smile. "Esmeira has that effect on people—makes them realise the potential within themselves."

As their journey continued, Alex's proficiency in using the Dimensional Communicator Dippy grew. The device became an invaluable tool, allowing him to communicate with Vesta, Dippy, and even his friends back in his home world.

One day, while navigating the treacherous Crystal Caverns, Alex received a message from an unexpected source, Marcus! Alex briefly explained what he'd been up to.

"So, how's your secret mission going? You've been MIA for weeks!"

Alex chuckled, typing a reply on the holographic keypad of the communicator.

"Hey, bro! Sorry about that, I've been caught up in this crazy adventure. Trust me, you wouldn't believe the things I've seen"

"Try me! Seriously, though, we miss you here. Scarlette and I have been wondering where you disappeared to" muttered Marcus.

Alex responded "I promise I'll fill you in on everything once I'm back. It's been... beyond anything I could have imagined"

"Can't wait to hear the details but remember, you've got a life here too. Don't forget about us while you're off saving the dimensions!"

"Haha, I won't and hey, tell Scarlette I said hi!", As Alex finished typing, he couldn't help but feel a pang of longing for his friends and his world.

He was grateful for the adventure, for the friendships he'd formed, but he missed the simplicity of his old life. Still, he knew that he couldn't turn back now. The fate of Esmeira depended on him, and he couldn't let Vesta down.

Alex knew it was time to return to his world. He bid farewell to his newfound friends, promising that he would always cherish the memories of Esmeira.

Back in his room, Alex looked around, feeling a mix of nostalgia and contentment.

It almost felt surreal that his extraordinary journey had been real.

He glanced at the Dimensional Communicator Dippy on his desk and smiled.

Even though the adventures were over, a part of him would always be connected to the realms beyond.

As he lay down to sleep, he wondered what the future held for him. Perhaps his life wouldn't be as ordinary as he had once thought.

With the memories of Esmeira and the friends he had made, Alex knew that he was ready to face whatever challenges lay ahead.

And so, with the echoes of distant dimensions in his heart, Alex Knight drifted into dreams, forever changed by an adventure that had taken him beyond the boundaries of his imagination.

Alex found himself settling back into his routine in his home world. Yet, the memories of Esmeira lingered like a vivid dream. He often found himself gazing at Dippy the Dimensional Communicator, wondering if there would ever be another call to adventure. Alex then typed a message to Vesta:

"I'm ready to help, Vesta. Esmeira's safety is my responsibility too."

"Alex, your determination is admirable. The rifts between dimensions may be sealed, but the threads of destiny continue to weave. Prepare yourself, for a new journey that awaits you." Vesta replied.

As the message ended, a portal of light opened in Alex's room. He knew that stepping through that portal would mark the beginning of another adventure a journey to protect dimensions and uphold the balance between realms.

With a deep breath and a sense of purpose, Alex stepped through the portal, leaving behind his ordinary life once more.

The portal closed behind him, leaving nothing but a sense of anticipation in the air.

Luckily with the help of "Guide to Worlds" he managed to be transported back home into his bedroom before his parents came back from work and the next day he would transport himself back to a new adventure. He needn't worry about school as they were currently on holidays but he hadn't seen his friends in a while due to these adventures. As much fun as he was having he surely did miss them but the people of Esmeira and the countless dimensions beyond were relying on him.

So, Alex Knight, armed with his newfound courage and the memories of his past victories, embarked on a journey that would take him through uncharted territories and unfamiliar worlds.

With Dippy, the Dimensional Communicator at his side and his heart filled with determination, he set forth to face whatever challenges awaited him.

The inter dimensional adventure had begun anew, and the hero within Alex was ready to shine once again.

The portal deposited him in a realm that seemed both familiar and different. The air crackled with energy, and the sky shimmered with hues of blue and gold.

Before him stood Lyra, a confident smirk on her face. "Fancy seeing you here, hero."

Alex grinned back, glad to have a familiar face by his side.

"I guess we're in this together once more."

Dippy zoomed around, his pixelated wings a blur.

"Oh, this is exciting! A brand-new dimension to explore!"

Lyra raised an eyebrow. "Dippy's energy is almost infectious."

The trio set off, navigating through a landscape that was a blend of magic and technology.

As they walked, Alex couldn't shake off the feeling that they were being watched. Suddenly, a figure emerged from the shadows, revealing himself to be a humanoid creature with ethereal, shifting features.

"Greetings, " the figure spoke, his voice echoing like ripples in a pond.

"I am Zephyrus, the Guardian of the Nexus."

Alex felt a sense of awe and curiosity. "The Nexus? What's that?"

Zephyrus gestured to the swirling vortex nearby.

"The Nexus is a crossroads of dimensions—a hub that connects realms and allows for the exchange of knowledge and ideas. But it seems that the balance of the Nexus is threatened."

Lyra crossed her arms, her expression serious. "By what?"

Zephyrus' features flickered with concern. "We suspect a being known as Vezan, the same individual who sought the Ancient Sacred Sceptre,

Now seeks to control the Nexus. With its power under his command, he could manipulate dimensions at will, causing chaos beyond measure."

Alex clenched his fists, remembering the battles he need a face. "We can't let that happen."

Dippy buzzed with determination. "Let's give him a pixel-perfect welcome!"

Zephyrus smiled warmly. "Your resolve is commendable.

But defeating Vezan won't be easy. His authority over dimensions makes him a formidable foe."

Alex smirked. "I've faced impossible odds before. We'll find a way."

From traversing shifting landscapes to deciphering ancient riddles, every obstacle was a test of their strength, teamwork, and determination.

Through it all, Alex and Lyra's bond grew stronger. They learned each other's strengths and weaknesses, complementing each other in battles and strategising together during moments of uncertainty.

Dippy's quick thinking often proved to be a lifesaver, his pixel-based magic weaving seamlessly into the fabric of their adventures.

One day, as they approached the heart of the Nexus, the portal hummed to life, ready to transport them back. As they stepped through, Alex glanced at Lyra, a grin tugging at his lips.

"Who would've thought our adventures would continue like this?"

Lyra smirked. "Life's a funny thing, isn't it?"

Dippy chimed in with his signature energy. "And we're ready to dive into the next level.

The portal closed, leaving nothing behind but the echoes of their inter-dimensional journey.

Back in his world, Alex found himself standing once again in his familiar location with the Ancient book Vesta gave him in is small pouch.

CHAPTER THREE

THE GUIDE TO WORLDS

"Hey guys, come on in!" smiled Alex cheerfully as he opened the door. "Alex Knight." Scarlette frowned as they made their way to his bedroom. "You gave us the worst ever fright of our lives."

"Yeah." Marcus added. "Weeks ago it seemed like you vanished into thin air just like that when we were already looking for you"

Alex explained everything.

"So now you're back again and you're telling us all about some strange dreams that you had." Scarlette's voice was a mix of concern and irritation as she almost pressed her angry face against Alex's.

"It wasn't a dream." Alex shook his head "and the Queen told me not to tell anyone about it but you two are my best friends, and I can't save the world without you."

Marcus chuckled. "Save the world? You must have left your brain behind when you got back."

"Laugh all you want." Alex grinned and reached into his pocket, producing a device. "But it's all true."

"What's that?" Marcus peered at it. "A new phone?"

"Yeah, it's a D-Phone." Alex grinned at his friends' puzzled expressions.

"D-Phone?" Scarlette and Marcus exchanged confused glances.

"A Dimension Phone," Alex replied. "It hooks up to the main dimensional transport centre and guides me through the dimensions."

"That would be great..." Marcus laughed. "If we could understand what any of that meant."

"W-ell." A squeaky voice sounded from the D-Phone. "Why don't I just show how this works, to allow you slow-minded mortals to catch up?"

"What the?" Scarlette and Marcus stared at the phone in Alex's hand, taken aback by the unexpected voice.

"Don't mind Dippy, He got a personality all of his own." Alex laughed. "Now come on, let's go on an adventure of a lifetime."

With a mixture of excitement and trepidation, Alex unclipped a small pouch from his belt, and from within, he carefully held the "Guide to Worlds before him, its pages seemingly infused with subtle, shimmering energy.

Vesta's words echoed in his mind, guiding his actions. "When you open the book," she had instructed, "read the magic words inscribed within, and the portal to Esmeira will open."

Taking a deep breath, Alex's fingers brushed against the book's ancient pages, the parchment crackling slightly beneath his touch. His friends watched with bated breath as he flipped open the book, revealing the text written in an elegant script that seemed to shift and shimmer like living ink.

The words were a series of magical rhymes, woven together in a rhythm that resonated with the very essence of magic. Alex's heart raced as he began to read aloud the magic words inscribed within, the syllables flowing from his lips like a song that had been etched into his very soul.

"*Umbrae inter mundos, spirita ab aeternitate,*

Porta patefacere ad Esmeira, ianuam aperire."

"*Ventus Lumen Esmeira.*"

As the final words left his mouth, a wave of energy swept through the surroundings, the air around them seemed to tremble,

a golden light emanating from the pages of the book. The words he had spoken reverberated through the fabric of reality, echoing across dimensions. In an instant, the world around them shifted. The ground beneath their feet quivered, and the very air crackled with energy.

Within moments, the world around them began to shift, colours melding into a vibrant dance of light. The sensation was like getting lost in the pages of an enchanting story, each word carrying them into a new realm.

When the shimmering light faded, the three friends found themselves transported to a land that could only be described as a fusion of fairy tale and comic book a realm where imagination became reality, and the extraordinary was an everyday occurrence.

Alex's heart raced with a mixture of exhilaration and uncertainty as he looked at his friends, their eyes filled with a mix of excitement and determination. The portal before they beckoned, offering a glimpse of a realm that held the key to their destiny

"Wow!" Marcus said with his mouth open. "This is better than any video game ever."

Scarlette was too speechless to say anything, her eyes wide with wonder.

"I told you so." Alex grinned and pointed at a bustling central station. "Look there, that's the central hub for traveling to all the dimensions there are."

"How do you know all this?" Scarlette finally found her voice, still trying to process the breath-taking scene before her.

"The Overseer of this place, Vesta, showed me around the first time I got here," Alex replied to his awestruck friends.

"Look there, those trains that look like they're on roller-coaster tracks. Each train can take you to another dimension.

The trains are decorated to represent the dimension they are going to. Look at that one..."

"That train looks like it's covered in candy canes and toffees." Marcus exclaimed, captivated by the sight.

"Does that mean it's going to a dimension of candy and chocolate treats?" Scarlette's eyes lit up with excitement.

"It does indeed." Dippy chimed in with his snarky little voice. "Would you like to go there?"

"I'm not too sure," Scarlette replied, her excitement tempered by caution. "Where are the other trains going?"

"To all the other dimensions, my dear." Dippy sang. "But Queen Vesta is going to be very cross if you outlanders go traipsing around dimensions. It may sound like fun, but it's very dangerous, you know."

"Oh, I'm sure we can look after ourselves," Alex said with unwavering confidence.

"After all, Vesta herself said I was chosen for greatness."

"Yes, yes, I suppose she did," Dippy said sourly. "But you all need proper equipment, you see, to look after yourselves."

"That looks like a place where we can get some equipment." Marcus pointed to what appeared to be a shop filled with an eclectic assortment of items.

"Right." Alex clapped his hands with determination. "Let's go in there and get what we need."

The shop's interior was a riot of colour and wonder, a place where the extraordinary met the practical. Alex led his friends down the aisle, inspecting the wares displayed before them. Their eyes fell upon a collection of weapons, gadgets, and tools.

"Look. That's a D-Blaster," Alex remarked, pointing at a sleek silver-purple handgun that bore an uncanny resemblance to a toy super soaker.

"Would that be a dimension blaster?" Scarlette asked, her curiosity piqued.

"Right, you are, Miss." A salesman in a flamboyant orange suit and a jaunty yellow hat appeared before them. "The best make and model—a very accurate and powerful choice. One shot is all it takes."

"Nice." Alex nodded. "We'll take three."

"Excellent." The salesman's nod matched his grin. "Would you like them packed for travel?"

"No need." Alex grinned back. "We'll just carry them with us as is."

"Very good, young sir. That will be three hundred Silver Ghost coins."

"What are Silver Ghost coins?" Alex's brow furrowed in perplexity.

"The cost for the D-Blasters." The salesman replied. "A hundred Silver Ghost coins each."

"But... we don't have any." Alex's shoulders slumped.

"You can earn Silver Ghost coins." Dippy interjected.

"How?" Alex and Marcus exchanged hopeful glances.

"By completing tasks in other dimensions." Dippy provided a solution. "You can also earn large ghost coins too or as I like to call them Power coins!" Dippy smiled. "Power Coins?" Alex asked curiously. "Indeed! These coins are earned depending on the task and when you get a powerful large silver ghost coin you have to rub it a few times and it will give you temporary powers!" Dippy said excitedly "However its powers are limited so you must not overuse it and you have to allow it re-charge otherwise if you do overuse it unfortunately it will drain you of its powers and turn you into an evil version of yourself temporarily…although I do not know why it would do this but you can also gain other useful items of the dimensions too!"

"Wow!" Marcus said in shock.

"Do you know a dimension where we can get them?" Scarlette inquired.

"Yes, there are a few indeed." Dippy's tone remained unchanging as if she had been expecting the question.

"Then what are we waiting for?" Alex's enthusiasm reignited. "The trains are all there. Let's get on one."

With a renewed sense of purpose, the trio embarked on their next adventure.

They boarded a train that was adorned with intricate patterns of swirling colours, a hint at the realm it would transport them to. The train's interior was just as enchanting and fashioned with materials and windows that seemed to display glimpses of different worlds.

As the train started moving, the landscapes outside shifted like a kaleidoscope, merging one into another in a whirlwind of colours and shapes.

Scarlette, Alex, and Marcus exchanged excited glances, their hearts racing with anticipation.

"According to Dippy, we need to complete tasks in different dimensions to earn Silver Ghost coins. It's our ticket to acquiring those D-Blasters." Alex explained.

"So, what's our first task then?" asked Scarlette.

"I've identified a dimension known as Arachnidia. It's a world inhabited by giant scorpions, and they require help. A swarm of venomous insects has been threatening their silk production, and they're willing to reward anyone who can rid them of this menace." Dippy answered.

"Giant scorpions and venomous insects? This is starting to sound like a very different kind of adventure." said Marcus worryingly.

"Well, it's a dimension like no other. Let's do this" replied Alex determinedly.

The train's rhythmic motion eventually came to a gentle halt, and the trio disembarked onto the terrain of Arachnidia. The landscape was dominated by towering trees with intricate webs woven between their branches. The air was thick with a sense of both danger and anticipation.

"So, where are these giant scorpions?" Scarlette asked looking around concernedly.

"Follow me, and I'll guide you to their lair" replied Dippy.

Through the web-covered forest, the trio ventured, guided by Dippy's navigation.

Their path led them deeper into the heart of Arachnidia, until they finally reached a clearing where a group of giant scorpions had gathered.

Marcus and Scarlette both held back a shriek.

"Greetings, we've come to offer our assistance with the insect problem." Alex said bravely.

The scorpions regarded them with a mix of curiosity and scepticism. Their eyes blinked in unison, assessing the newcomers.

Scorpion Elder looked reluctantly, "You're not native to Arachnidia. What makes you think you can help?"

"We've faced challenges before, and we're determined to earn Silver Ghost coins to acquire equipment that will benefit us in our journey." Alex answered confidently.

"Plus, we're not afraid to lend a hand when it's needed." Marcus replied nervously.

The Scorpion Elder observed them for a moment before nodding in agreement.

"Very well. If you can eradicate the swarm of venomous insects that threaten our silk production, we'll reward you with Silver Ghost coins."

The trio accepted the task with determination. Armed with makeshift weapons they had acquired earlier, they ventured deeper into the forest, their senses heightened as they remained on the lookout for signs of the menacing insects.

Hours turned into a tense search, as the trio encountered various challenges along the way.

The venomous insects were no ordinary foes they could camouflage themselves seamlessly, making them difficult to detect. Scarlette's agility, Alex's quick thinking, and Marcus's ingenuity were put to the test as they navigated the dangerous landscape.

Alex, "I've got an idea. We'll create a trap using these sticky tree sap blobs. When the insects come to feed, they'll get stuck."

"Good thinking. Let's gather as much sap as we can Marcus."

Working together, they set up their trap and waited. As the insects were drawn to the scent of the sap, they became ensnared, their movements slowed by the sticky substance "Now!"

(*With precise timing, the trio sprang into action, delivering swift blows to the immobilised insects. Their combined efforts proved successful, and the threat to the scorpions' silk production was eradicated.*)

Upon returning to the scorpions' clearing, the Scorpion Elder acknowledged their triumph.

"You have proven your worth. We are grateful for your assistance" said the Scorpion elder.

"Thank you. In return, we would greatly appreciate Silver Ghost coins."

The Scorpion Elder extended its front claws, releasing shiny and transparent small shiny silver coins. The trio collected the coins, feeling a sense of accomplishment as they realised they were one step closer to acquiring the D-Blasters.

As they left Arachnidia and returned to the central station, Dippy's voice sounded once more from the D-Phone.

Dippy voiced, "Congratulations! You've completed your first task and earned Silver Ghost coins. Your determination and courage will serve you well on this journey." "We did it!" Alex beamed. They all jumped excitedly hugging each other.

With their newfound coins in hand and a sense of camaraderie, the trio gazed upon the array of trains before them—each representing a new adventure, a new challenge. "So, what do you say we hop on another train and continue our quest?" Marcus asked excitedly.

"Absolutely. We've barely scratched the surface of what these dimensions hold." said Alex smiling.

"Let's make the most of this opportunity. The worlds are waiting for us." Scarlette added brightly.

As they boarded a train bound for their next destination, the sense of wonder and excitement remained unabated. With every journey to a new dimension, they were writing their own story—one of courage, friendship, and the unwavering belief that within the pages of their adventures, greatness awaited.

The train ride was a chance for them to reflect on their accomplishments and speculate about the challenges that lay ahead. Each dimension they encountered had its unique landscape, inhabitants, and trials. From the serene beauty of Celestial Isle, where ethereal creatures resided, to the puzzling labyrinthine world of Enigmaria, where riddles were the currency of progression, their experiences only fuelled their determination to succeed.

"Isn't it incredible how each dimension is like a separate universe of its own, Alex?"

"It's like every time we step off the train, we're stepping into a whole new story and we're the protagonists in every one of them." Marcus said in awe.

After completing tasks in various dimensions, they accumulated a collection of Silver Ghost coins. These tasks had not only tested their skills but also strengthened their bond as friends. The coins served as a symbol of their progress and a reminder of the challenges they had overcome.

As they stood in the central station, gazing at the trains before them, Dippy's voice piped up from the D-Phone.

"Greetings, adventurers. I have an update for you."

"What's up, Dippy?" Alex asked with bowl of curiosity on his face

"I've received information about a dimension known as Chronosanct. It's a realm of time manipulation, where the flow of time is malleable."

"That sounds intriguing!" said Scarlette.

"Indeed, the inhabitants of Chronosanct are seeking assistance to mend a tear in the fabric of time. It's a challenge that requires a delicate touch and an understanding of the temporal arts"

"Time manipulation? This could be our most challenging task yet." Marcus wondered

"It's a risk worth taking. Let's check it out!" smiled Alex.

The train that would transport them to Chronosanct awaited, its design reminiscent of a clockwork masterpiece. As they boarded, they knew they were embarking on an adventure that could reshape their perception of reality itself.

In Chronosanct, the trio was met by a guide named Tempora, a figure cloaked in shimmering robes that seemed to ripple like the surface of the water.

"Welcome, travellers. I sense you possess the potential to mend the temporal tear that plagues our realm. Tempora welcomed them"

"We're honoured to help. How can we mend this tear?

"To mend the tear, you must navigate the Chronogrove—a maze of shifting timelines. Solve the riddles that guard the path, and you will reach the heart of the tear."

The Chronogrove was a labyrinth of pathways that seemed to bend and twist according to its own rhythm. Riddles were inscribed on plaques at intersections, each riddle a clue to the correct path.

The trio embarked on this intricate puzzle, their minds challenged by the riddles and their determination unwavering. With each solved riddle, they felt they were getting closer to their goal.

As they reached the heart of the tear, they were met with a scene of temporal chaos. Threads of time intertwined and clashed, creating a spectacle of discord.

"You must channel your collective will and focus it on the tear. In unity, you can mend the fabric of time."

Pooling their resolve, Scarlette, Alex, and Marcus reached out to the tear, their touch a testament to their friendship and their shared purpose. With a surge of energy, the tear began to mend, the threads of time reweaving into harmony.

"You have done it. You have restored balance to Chronosanct." Tempora altered.

As the tear mended, the very landscape of Chronosanct transformed. Tempora nodded in approval, acknowledging their success.

"For your service, I offer you these Temporal Tokens—a currency of time itself. Use them wisely."

With the Temporal Tokens in their possession, the trio returned to the central station, triumphant in their accomplishment. As they contemplated their next move, Dippy's voice resonated from the D-Phone.

"You've demonstrated exceptional valour and resourcefulness in Chronosanct. Your journey continues to unfold, and the dimensions await your presence."

"Thank you, Dippy" Alex said gladly. "We're ready for whatever comes next."

With their Temporal Tokens in hand and the sense of accomplishment still fresh, they turned their attention to the array of trains before them. Each train was a gateway to a new adventure, a new dimension with its trials and triumphs.

"Every time we complete a task and earn these coins, it's like we're rewriting the rules of these dimensions." Alex said proudly

"And leaving our mark on their stories." replied Marcus

"Exactly. And in the process, we're growing stronger, both as individuals and as a team." Scarlette added.

With a shared determination, they selected a train that would take them to their next destination—an uncharted world awaiting their presence. As they stepped onto the train, they felt the rush of excitement that came with embracing the unknown.

In this new dimension, known as Phantasmagoria, they encountered an ethereal realm where reality itself seemed to shift and change.

Illusions and dreams intermingled, blurring the line between imagination and reality.

Their task in Phantasmagoria was to solve a series of enigmatic puzzles set by the Dreamweaver's, mystical beings who wove the fabric of dreams.

Dreamweaver addressed them with hope in her voice, "Welcome, travellers. The puzzles you solve will shape the dreamscape and guide us toward harmony."

As they delved into the puzzles, the trio found themselves navigating landscapes that defied the laws of physics. Bridges turned into rainbows, and mirrors reflected not just images but fragments of their thoughts.

"This place is like a living puzzle itself." Marcus said looking around confusedly.

"And solving it will restore balance to the Dreamweavers' realm." Scarlette replied.

"Let's put our heads together and crack these puzzles." Alex said determined.

Through trial and error, deduction, and a dash of creative thinking, they unravelled the enigmas one by one. With each solved puzzle, the realm of Phantasmagoria transformed, revealing new paths and possibilities.

A wise Dreamweaver acknowledged their efforts "You have proven your worth, and the dreamscape resonates with your actions."

With their task complete, they were rewarded with Dreamshards—shimmering fragments of the dreamscape itself.

The Dreamweavers explained that these shards held unique properties and could be harnessed for various purposes.

As they left Phantasmagoria and returned to the central station, Dippy's voice greeted them.

Dippy added, "Congratulations! The dreamscape now echoes your achievements. Your journey continues to inspire."

With Dreamshards in their possession and a sense of accomplishment warming their hearts, the trio faced the trains once more. Each train offered a chance to embark on a new adventure, explore uncharted territories, and make a difference in the dimensions they encountered.

Alex grinned, "Our quest is far from over. Every dimension we visit is like a chapter in our own story."

Scarlette added, "And we're the authors of our own destiny."

Marcus mused, "So, where shall we go next?"

As they boarded another train, bound for yet another dimension, they knew that their journey was one of boundless potential, of challenges met with courage, and of friendship that grew stronger with each trial.

Scarlette mused, "I wonder what kind of world awaits us this time."

Marcus grinned, "Who knows? But one thing's for sure—it's going to be an adventure."

"Agreed. Let's embrace it fully" replied Alex.

With a sense of anticipation and excitement, they watched as the landscape outside the train transformed. The scenery shifted, colours danced, and before they knew it, they had arrived at their next destination—Veridian Vale.

Veridian Vale was a lush and vibrant land, a paradise of flora and fauna. The air was filled with the melodious songs of exotic birds, and the fragrance of blooming flowers permeated every corner.

Their task in Veridian Vale was to aid the Nature keepers, guardians of the land who sought to maintain the delicate balance of nature.

The Nature keepers' harmony had been disrupted by the intrusion of a powerful, unnatural force.

Nature keeper Elysia welcomed the trio, "Travellers, your arrival is a sign that hope remains. The balance of Veridian Vale must be restored."

As they ventured into the heart of the vale, they encountered creatures both marvellous and mysterious.

The trio put their heads together and came up with a plan to coax the Luminis Butterflies into following them as they were heading towards the threat and the butterflies illuminated the powerful unnatural dark force with their radiant wings, while the Verdant Drakes soared through the sky, leaving trails of emerald light ultimately defeating the unnatural force which was on the verge of causing major destruction to the Vale. "My dear friends, I thank you so much for restoring balance to the Vale" Elysia smiled gratefully and the trio were rewarded with a jar of the Luminis Butterflies.

Alex mused as they returned to the central station, "Every dimension we visit leaves its mark on us, and we leave our mark on it."

Scarlette added, "Yeah, It's a beautiful exchange."

Marcus concluded, "And countless more stories are waiting to be written."

With shared purpose and unwavering determination, they stepped onto the next train, ready to embrace the challenges and marvels of the dimension that awaited them.

Scarlette's curiosity couldn't be contained, "I can't help but wonder what other dimensions have in store for us."

Marcus chimed in, "Each one has been so unique and unexpected."

Alex affirmed, "And it's a privilege to play a role in each dimension's story."

As the train journeyed on, the landscape outside the window shifted once more. Colours merged, and the environment transformed, announcing their arrival in their next destination, Prismara.

Prismara welcomed them to a realm of vivid colours and refracted light.

It was a breath-taking world where every breath they took seemed to shimmer with hues unknown to their home world.

Here, the inhabitants were Lumisprites small, luminous beings that radiated light and brought colour to their surroundings.

Their task in Prismara was to assist the Lumisprites in restoring the Prism Crystal, a source of radiant energy that had begun to lose its brilliance.

Lumisprite Aurora addressed them with a touch of sadness,

"Welcome, travellers. The Prism Crystal's light is fading, and our world is growing dim."

As they journeyed through Prismara's stunning landscapes, they encountered puzzles that challenged their perception of light and colours.

They utilised Prismara's unique properties to manipulate the elements of light, working together to restore the Prism Crystal's radiance.

Scarlette marvelled, "It's like we're inside a living rainbow."

Marcus added, "And every step we take adds to the brilliance of Prismara."

Alex concluded, "Let's work together to restore the Crystal's light."

Guided by the Lumisprites, they uncovered the source of the Prism Crystal's dimming a dark crystalline entity known as the Shadowquartz.

This entity fed on the Crystal's radiance, causing imbalance.

Their battle against the Shadowquartz tested their strategy and determination. They harnessed the power of light, reflecting it off surfaces to weaken the entity's defences. As the battle raged on, the landscape itself responded to their efforts, colours intensifying and merging into dazzling displays.

Lumisprite Aurora acknowledged their valour,

"You are champions of light, and your efforts have rekindled our world's splendour."

With the defeat of the Shadowquartz, the Prism Crystal began to glow with renewed brilliance. Its light spread throughout Prismara, painting the world with a symphony of colours.

Lumisprite Aurora expressed her gratitude, "As tokens of our gratitude, we bestow upon you Radiant Shards—fragments of Prismara's essence."

Radiant Shards held the very essence of Prismara's light. They possessed the power to create prismatic illusions, illuminate darkness, and conjure ephemeral rainbows. The shards were a testament to the trio's role in rejuvenating Prismara's vitality.

As they left Prismara, Dippy's voice resonated from the D-Phone. "Prismara's colours shine brighter thanks to your efforts. Your journey continues to paint the dimensions with your deeds."

With Radiant Shards in their possession and a sense of accomplishment warming their hearts, the trio once again faced the choice of trains. Each train symbolised a fresh opportunity, a new adventure, and a chance to make a positive impact on the dimensions they encountered.

"Our journey is a mosaic of experiences, each piece adding to the grand tapestry." Said Alex.

Scarlette added, "And it's a tapestry that reflects our growth and unity."

With excitement in their hearts and a shared sense of purpose, they stepped onto the next train, ready to uncover the mysteries, face the challenges, and embrace the wonders of the next dimension that awaited them.

Scarlette wondered aloud, "It's amazing how each world we visit has its unique magic."

The train journey continued, and as they gazed out the window, the scenery transformed once again. Colours blended, and the environment reshaped, announcing their arrival in a realm known as Mechanika.

Mechanika was a world of gears, steam, and invention. Mechanical wonders filled every corner, from clockwork creatures to steam-powered contraptions.

Their mission in Mechanika was clear—to assist the Gearwrights, ingenious engineers who maintained the delicate balance of the mechanical ecosystem. Disruptions had arisen due to the emergence of a powerful energy anomaly.

Gearwright Orion welcomed them with urgency, "Greetings, travellers. Our machines have been thrown into chaos by this anomaly."

As they explored Mechanika's intricate landscapes, they encountered Clockwork Critters—small, animated machines that brought both joy and challenge. These Critters were vital to Mechanika's infrastructure, but the anomaly had affected their behaviour.

Scarlette marvelled, "It's like stepping into a world of gears and cogs."

Marcus noted, "And every twist and turn of these machines is a piece of Mechanika's heartbeat."

Alex affirmed, "We're here to restore that heartbeat."

Guided by the Gear wrights, they faced puzzles that demanded their understanding of Mechanika's mechanics.

They navigated through gears, rerouted steam, and solved intricate patterns. Through their teamwork and knowledge, they sought to bring stability back to the mechanical world.

Gear wright Orion acknowledged their skill, "Your dedication is pivotal in restoring order to Mechanika."

By understanding the mechanics and recalibrating the Dissonance Engine—a contraption generating discordant energy—they restored harmony to the realm's machinery. The Clockwork Critters moved in unison, and Mechanika's mechanical symphony played once more.

Gear wright Orion expressed his gratitude, "You've set the gears of Mechanika back in motion."

With the Dissonance Engine restored Mechanika's machinery hummed with renewed precision. Their efforts not only fixed the mechanics but also contributed to the realm's harmonious song.

As they left Mechanika, Dippy's voice echoed through the D-Phone. "Mechanika's mechanics run smoothly thanks to your expertise. Your journey continues to shape the dimensions."

With Steamheart Cores in their possession and a sense of accomplishment warming their hearts, the trio once again faced the array of trains. Each train beckoned with the promise of new adventures, opportunities to learn, and chances to contribute to the dimensions they visited.

With a shared sense of purpose and excitement, they stepped onto the next train, ready to immerse themselves in the challenges and marvels of the next dimension.

Scarlette wondered, "It's like venturing into a realm where every colour is a note, and every step is a musical phrase."

Marcus agreed, "And our presence adds new verses to the eternal song of Harmonica."

Alex added, "Every dimension is a stanza, and we're the lyricists of our melodious tale."

As the train journeyed forward, the landscape outside the window transformed once more. Colours merged, and the environment reshaped, announcing their arrival in a realm that appeared both ancient and futuristic Chronoterra.

Chronoterra was a world where time was both malleable and tangible. Clock towers reached into the sky, and streams of flowing time cascaded through the landscape.

Their task in Chronoterra was to aid the Chronomancers, guardians of temporal stability who managed the ebb and flow of time's currents. Disturbances in time had begun to cause rifts and anomalies.

Chronomancer Selene addressed them with urgency, "Greetings, travellers. Time's tapestry is unravelling, and we seek your assistance."

As they explored Chronoterra's dynamic landscapes, they encountered Temporal Guardians—beings that embodied different eras of history. From ancient warriors to futuristic explorers, these guardians held key points in time.

Scarlette marvelled, "This place is like a living history book."

Marcus noted, "And every page we turn reveals a new mystery."

Alex affirmed, "Our role is to restore the missing pages and mend the tapestry."

Guided by the Chronomancers, they faced temporal puzzles that challenged their understanding of cause and effect. They traversed eras that seamlessly flowed into one another, mending time's fractures as they went.

Chronomancer Selene acknowledged their efforts, "Your determination is the thread that weaves time's fabric back together."

Through careful manipulation and skilful use of time, they worked to mend the rifts and stabilise the timeline. They confronted the Temporal Anomaly a vortex of distorted time and together, they restored its equilibrium.

Chronomancer Selene praised their bravery, "You are guardians of time, and your efforts have safeguarded Chronoterra's history."

With the Temporal Anomaly pacified, Chronoterra's flow of time regained its harmony. Clock towers chimed in unison, and the realm resonated with echoes from the past, present, and future.

Chronomancer Selene expressed her gratitude, "As tokens of our gratitude, we offer you Time crystal Shardsfragments that resonate with the essence of time."

Time crystal Shards possessed the power to manipulate time within limits, speeding up or slowing down events, and even glimpsing into moments that had passed. They were a testament to the trio's role in preserving the continuity of Chronoterra's history.

As they left Chronoterra, Dippy's voice echoed from the D-Phone. "Time's tapestry is richer due to your interventions. Your journey continues to weave the dimensions."

With Time crystal Shards in their possession and a sense of accomplishment warming their hearts, the trio once again faced the choice of trains. Each train offered a chance to explore, learn, and shape the dimensions they would encounter.

Alex mused, "Our journey is a chronicle of experiences, each moment contributing to the grand narrative."

With a shared sense of purpose and eager anticipation, they stepped onto the next train, ready to unravel the mysteries, confront the challenges, and savour the wonders of the next dimension that awaited them.

Scarlette wondered, "What if time is like a river, and our actions are the pebbles that create ripples?"

Marcus agreed, "And as those ripples spread, they reshape the riverbanks of Temporaqua."

Alex added, "Every dimension is a watershed, and we're the stewards of our own aqueous saga."

As the train journeyed on, the landscape outside the window shifted once more. Colours blended, and the environment transformed, announcing their arrival in their next destination Temporaqua.

Temporaqua was a world of fluidity and change. Rivers of time flowed through the land, and waterfalls cascaded with shimmering droplets that held memories of moments long past.

Their mission in Temporaqua was clear to assist the Aquachrons, guardians of the aquatic realm who maintained the balance of time within water's embrace. Disruptions had arisen due to the disturbance of Temporaqua's temporal currents.

Aquachron Marina addressed them with resolve, "Greetings, travellers. The currents of time are turbulent, and we seek your aid in restoring tranquillity."

As they explored Temporaqua's aquatic landscapes, they encountered Elemental Naiads—water spirits that embodied the essence of the realm's waters. Each Naiad held a different aspect of Temporaqua's history and character.

Scarlette marvelled, "It's like diving into a sea of memories."

Alex affirmed, "Our task is to mend those ripples and bring harmony back to the currents."

Guided by the Aquachrons, they faced water-themed puzzles that required their understanding of the interplay between time and fluidity. They traversed currents that shifted as they moved, encountering puzzles that demanded quick thinking and cooperation.

Aquachron Marina praised their adaptability,

"Your determination is like water's flow unyielding yet ever-changing."

By manipulating the currents and navigating Temporaqua's aqueous mazes, they aimed to restore stability to the realm's time-woven waters. They confronted the Chrono Cascade—a torrent of time's energy and through their combined efforts, they tamed its turbulent flow.

Aquachron Marina expressed her gratitude, "You are champions of the aquatic realm, and your actions have brought serenity back to Temporaqua."

With the Chrono Cascade stilled Temporaqua's rivers flowed with tranquil grace. Waterfalls glistened with the memories of moments preserved in time, and the aquatic realm resonated with harmony.

Aquachron Marina offered tokens of appreciation, "As symbols of our gratitude, we present you with Tidewater Gems. Gems that reflect the essence of water's embrace."

Tidewater Gems possessed the power to manipulate water within limits, conjuring streams, forming barriers, and even glimpsing into moments suspended in the currents. They were a testament to the trio's role in safeguarding Temporaqua's temporal waters.

As they left Temporaqua, Dippy's voice echoed from the D-Phone. "Temporaqua's waters now mirror your interventions. Your journey continues to shape the dimensions."

With Tidewater Gems in their possession and a sense of accomplishment warming their hearts, the trio once again faced the array of trains. Each train beckoned with the promise of new adventures, opportunities to learn, and chances to contribute to the dimensions they visited.

With shared purpose and unwavering determination, they stepped onto the next train, ready to embrace the challenges and marvels of the dimension that awaited them.

As the train journeyed on, the landscape beyond the windows transformed once more. Colours danced, and the environment reshaped, announcing their arrival in a realm shrouded in mist and mystery Enigmara.

Enigmara was a world of secrets and enigmas. Riddles and puzzles adorned the landscape, and every whisper of the wind seemed to carry hidden messages.

Their mission in Enigmara was clear to assist the Riddle keepers, guardians of the realm who safeguarded its knowledge and guarded its secrets. The balance of Enigmara had been disrupted by the fading of ancient riddles.

Riddle keeper Orion addressed them with a cryptic smile, "Greetings, travellers. The answers to our riddles have been lost to time. We beseech your aid in restoring their essence."

As they explored Enigmara's misty landscapes, they encountered Shrouded Sages wisdom-keepers who held fragments of the realm's ancient knowledge. The sages were veiled in mystery, and unlocking their insights required unravelling their riddles.

Scarlette marvelled, "It's like walking through a world of hidden meanings."

Marcus noted, "And every puzzle we solve is like lifting a veil from reality's face."

Alex affirmed, "Our role is to illuminate the hidden truths and restore the realm's equilibrium."

Guided by the Riddle keepers, they unravelled intricate riddles that demanded their intuition and lateral thinking. Each solved puzzle revealed a piece of Enigmara's forgotten wisdom, contributing to the restoration of its ancient truths.

Riddle keeper Orion commended their insight, "Your minds are like keys that unlock the doors of Enigmara's mysteries."

By deciphering the enigmatic riddles and unveiling the essence of the realm's knowledge, they aimed to restore the equilibrium that had been disrupted. They confronted the Enigma Nexus a puzzle of profound complexity and through their combined wisdom, they unravelled its intricacies.

Riddle keeper Orion expressed his gratitude, "You are true seekers of truth, and your actions have rekindled Enigmara's enlightenment."

With the Enigma Nexus resolved, Enigmara's realm echoed with the whispers of forgotten riddles restored to their rightful place. Hidden passages opened, and the mist that shrouded the

realm began to dissipate.

Riddle keeper Orion offered tokens of appreciation, "As tokens of gratitude, we present you with Echo Crystals that resonate with the essence of mysteries unveiled."

Echo Crystals possessed the power to echo and amplify sounds within limits, unveil concealed truths, and even grant glimpses into the hidden layers of reality.

They were a testament to the trio's role in restoring Enigmara's enigmatic equilibrium.

As they left Enigmara, Dippy's voice echoed from the D-Phone. "Enigmara's mysteries echo with your interventions. Your journey continues to shape the dimensions."

With Echo Crystals in their possession and a sense of accomplishment warming their hearts, the trio once more faced the choice of trains. Each train symbolised a fresh opportunity, a new adventure, and a chance to make a positive impact on the dimensions they encountered.

With a shared sense of purpose and excitement, they stepped onto the next train, ready to uncover the mysteries, face the challenges, and embrace the wonders of the next dimension that awaited them.

Scarlette wondered, "What if the realm we visit is like a canvas, and every action we take is a brushstroke?"

Marcus agreed, "And our presence adds colour to the world of Chromatica."

Alex added, "Every dimension is a palette, and we're the artists of our vibrant journey."

As the train journeyed forward, the landscape outside the window transformed once more. Colours blended, and the environment reshaped, announcing their arrival in a realm that seemed like a living painting Chromatica.

Chromatica was a world of vivid colours and artistic wonders. The landscapes were alive with brushstrokes of light and hue, and the air resonated with the melodies of harmonious pigments.

Their task in Chromatica was clear to assist the Chromaphiles, creators who imbued the realm with their artistic essence. Disruptions had arisen due to the fading of the realm's vibrant colours.

Chromaphile Celestia addressed them with determination, "Greetings, travellers. The colours of Chromatica are dimming, and we call upon your aid to restore their brilliance."

As they explored Chromatica's artistic landscapes, they encountered Palette Spirits ethereal beings that embodied the hues of the realm. Each Palette Spirit held a different colour aspect of Chromatica's vibrancy.

Scarlette marvelled, "It's like stepping into a world painted with magic."

Alex affirmed, "Our task is to bring back the colours and rekindle the realm's vibrancy."

Guided by the Chromaphiles, they faced colour-themed puzzles that required their understanding of hue, shade, and artistic expression. They blended colours, manipulated light, and restored pigments, aiming to return Chromatica to its radiant splendour.

Chromaphile Celestia acknowledged their creativity, "Your actions are strokes of brilliance that illuminate Chromatica's canvas."

By embracing their artistic intuition and cooperating with the Palette Spirits, they sought to restore the fading colours and reinvigorate the realm's artistic essence. They confronted the Chroma Anomaly a swirling vortex of colours and through their combined creative effort, they revitalised its chromatic harmony.

Chromaphile Celestia expressed her gratitude, "You are artists of the heart, and your efforts have breathed life into Chromatica's palette."

With the Chroma Anomaly pacified, Chromatica's landscapes burst with renewed vibrancy. Colours danced and intertwined, creating a symphony of visual wonder that painted the realm with a renewed artistic energy.

Chromaphile Celestia offered tokens of appreciation, "As symbols of our gratitude, we present you with Prismshards fragments that capture the essence of Chromatica's colours."

Prismshards possessed the power to manipulate and project colours within limits, creating breath-taking displays, unveiling hidden patterns, and even connecting with the emotions that colours evoked. They were a testament to the trio's role in revitalising Chromatica's artistic vibrancy.

As they left Chromatica, Dippy's voice echoed from the D-Phone. "Chromatica's canvas is richer due to your creative interventions. Your journey continues to shape the dimensions."

With Prismshards in their possession and a sense of accomplishment warming their hearts, the trio once again faced the array of trains. Each train beckoned with the promise of new adventures, opportunities to learn, and chances to contribute to the dimensions they visited.

With shared purpose and unwavering determination, they stepped onto the next train, ready to embrace the challenges and marvels of the dimension that awaited them.

As the train journeyed on, the landscape beyond the windows transformed once more. Colours merged, and the environment reshaped, announcing their arrival in a realm of light and shadows—Umbratica.

Umbratica was a world where darkness and light coexisted in delicate balance. Silhouettes danced in the shadows, and ethereal light illuminated the unseen.

Their mission in Umbratica was clear to assist the Umbralights, guardians of the realm who maintained the equilibrium between light and shadow. Disruptions had arisen due to the fading of Umbratica's luminance.

Umbralight Seraph addressed them with a solemn tone, "Greetings, travellers. The dance of light and shadow is losing its harmony, and we implore your help in restoring its balance."

As they explored Umbratica's interplay of light and shadow, they encountered Luminous Spirits beings that embodied the essence of both darkness and illumination. Each Luminous Spirit held a different facet of Umbratica's balance.

Scarlette marvelled, "It's like stepping into a world of contrasts and contradictions."

Marcus noted, "And every step we take adds to the tapestry of Umbratica's dual nature."

Alex affirmed, "Our role is to restore the equilibrium and rekindle the realm's luminescence."

Guided by the Umbra lights, they faced puzzles that demanded their understanding of the interplay between light and shadow. They manipulated light sources, unravelled optical illusions, and balanced darkness and illumination, seeking to restore Umbratica's harmony.

Umbra light Seraph praised their diligence, "Your persistence is like a beacon that guides Umbratica's balance."

By embracing both darkness and light and working together with the Luminous Spirits, they aimed to restore the fading equilibrium. They confronted the Equinox Convergence a point where light and shadow intertwined and through their combined efforts, they rekindled its delicate balance.

Umbralight Seraph expressed gratitude, "You are luminaries of harmony, and your actions have illuminated Umbratica's realm."

With the Equinox Convergence restored Umbratica's dance of light and shadow regained its mesmerising balance. Silhouettes danced with ethereal grace, and the realm resonated with the harmony of its dual nature.

Umbralight Seraph offered tokens of appreciation, "As tokens of our gratitude, we bestow upon you Luminary Cores. Cores that radiate the essence of Umbratica's equilibrium."

Luminary Cores possessed the power to manipulate light and shadow within limits, creating illusions, revealing hidden pathways, and even connecting with the essence of duality. They were a testament to the trio's role in preserving Umbratica's delicate balance.

As they left Umbratica, Dippy's voice echoed from the D-Phone. "Umbratica's dual nature is preserved due to your interventions. Your journey continues to shape the dimensions."

With Luminary Cores in their possession and a sense of accomplishment warming their hearts, the trio once more faced the choice of trains. Each train symbolised a fresh opportunity, a new adventure, and a chance to make a positive impact on the dimensions they encountered.

Scarlette wondered, "What if the realm we visit is like a garden, and every action we take is a seed?"

Marcus agreed, "And our presence nurtures the growth of Floraria."

As the train journeyed forward, the landscape outside the window transformed once more. Colours blended, and the environment reshaped, announcing their arrival in a realm of flora and botanical wonders Floraria.

Floraria was a world of lush greenery and vibrant blooms. Every step released fragrant scents, and the air was alive with the hum of pollinators.

Their task in Floraria was clear to assist the Botanists, guardians of the realm who nurtured the balance of its plant life. Disruptions had arisen due to the withering of Floraria's natural vitality.

Botanist Flora addressed them with a gentle smile, "Greetings, travellers. The harmony of Floraria's flora is fading, and we beseech your help in restoring its vibrancy."

As they explored Floraria's botanical landscapes, they encountered

Elemental Sprites spirits of nature that embodied the essence of the realm's plants. Each Elemental Sprite held a different facet of Floraria's vitality.

Scarlette marvelled, "It's like walking through a world of living gardens."

Alex affirmed, "Our role is to rekindle the realm's natural vitality and restore its equilibrium."

Guided by the Botanists, they faced plant-themed puzzles that required their understanding of growth, nurturing, and symbiosis. They cultivated gardens, directed water flows, and embraced the rhythms of nature, aiming to bring back Floraria's verdant splendour.

Botanist Flora praised their dedication, "Your efforts are like the sunlight that rejuvenates Floraria's heart."

By embracing their nurturing spirit and collaborating with the Elemental Sprites, they sought to restore the realm's vitality and reinvigorate its plant life. They confronted the Essence Eclipse a moment when life energy waned and through their combined efforts, they revitalised its natural balance.

Botanist Flora expressed her gratitude, "You are guardians of the green, and your actions have breathed life into Floraria's flora."

With the Essence Eclipse dispelled, Floraria's botanical landscapes burst forth with renewed vitality. Blossoms unfurled in vibrant displays, and the realm resonated with the harmonious rhythms of nature.

Botanist Flora offered tokens of appreciation, "As symbols of our gratitude, we present you with Sylvalite Seeds that hold the essence of Floraria's bloom."

Sylvanite Seeds possessed the power to nurture and manipulate plant life within limits, accelerating growth, summoning flora to aid them, and even connecting with the essence of natural cycles. They were a testament to the trio's role in preserving Floraria's botanical equilibrium.

As they left Floraria, Dippy's voice echoed from the D-Phone. "Floraria's gardens flourish due to your nurturing interventions. Your journey continues to shape the dimensions."

With Sylvalite Seeds in their possession and a sense of accomplishment warming their hearts, the trio once again faced the array of trains. Each train beckoned with the promise of new adventures, opportunities to learn, and chances to contribute to the dimensions they visited.

As the train journeyed on, the landscape beyond the windows transformed once more. Colours merged, and the environment reshaped, announcing their arrival in a realm where sound and silence harmonised Sonantia.

Sonantia was a world where melodies and rhythms interwoven in a symphony of creation. Sound waves danced in the air, and the very ground resonated with musical vibrations.

Their mission in Sonantia was clear to assist the Melodists, guardians of the realm who maintained the equilibrium between sound and silence. Disruptions had arisen due to the fading of Sonantia's harmonious melodies.

Melodist Aria addressed them with a melodic voice, "Greetings, travellers. The balance of sound and silence is shifting, and we seek your assistance in restoring its harmony."

As they explored Sonantia's realm of sound, they encountered Harmony Spirits ethereal beings that embodied the essence of melodies and rhythms. Each Harmony Spirit held a different aspect of Sonantia's musical balance.

Scarlette marvelled, "It's like stepping into a world of living symphonies."

Alex affirmed, "Our task is to restore the realm's harmony and rekindle its melodies."

Guided by the Melodists, they faced sound-themed puzzles that required their understanding of rhythm, pitch, and harmony. They composed melodies, synchronised echoes, and embraced the cadence of music, seeking to restore Sonantia's harmonious balance.

Melodist Aria praised their dedication, "Your efforts are like musical threads that weave Sonantia's tapestry."

By embracing their sense of harmony and working together with the Harmony Spirits, they aimed to rekindle the fading melodies and rejuvenate the realm's musical essence. They confronted the Resonance Disruption a discordant disturbance and through their combined musical prowess, they restored its harmonious equilibrium.

Melodist Aria expressed gratitude, "You are composers of balance, and your actions have reinvigorated Sonantia's melodies."

With the Resonance Disruption pacified, Sonantia's realm resonated once more with enchanting melodies. Every sound became a part of the symphony, and the air shimmered with the cadence of harmony.

Melodist Aria offered tokens of appreciation, "As symbols of our gratitude, we present you with Chord Crystals that hold the essence of Sonantia's melodies."

Chord Crystals possessed the power to manipulate and amplify sound within limits, creating harmonious arrangements, revealing hidden harmonies, and even connecting with the essence of resonance. They were a testament to the trio's role in preserving Sonantia's musical equilibrium.

As they left Sonantia, Dippy's voice echoed from the D-Phone. "Sonantia's melodies resonate with your harmonious interventions. Your journey continues to shape the dimensions."

With Chord Crystals in their possession and a sense of accomplishment warming their hearts, the trio once more faced the choice of trains. Each train symbolised a fresh opportunity, a new adventure, and a chance to make a positive impact on the dimensions they encountered.

Scarlette wondered, "What if the realm we visit is like a dream, and every action we take is a thought?"

Marcus agreed, "And our presence shapes the dreamscape of Somnia."

Alex added, "Every dimension is a realm of possibility, and we're the dreamers of our own visionary journey."

As the train journeyed forward, the landscape outside the window transformed once more. Colours blended, and the environment reshaped, announcing their arrival in a realm of imagination and fantasy Somnia.

Somnia was a world of dreams and wonder. Landscapes shifted like mirages, and the air was alive with ephemeral echoes of fantastical tales.

Their task in Somnia was clear to assist the Dreamweavers, guardians of the realm who wove the fabric of its dreamscape. Disruptions had arisen due to the unravelling of Somnia's imaginative threads. Dreamweaver Noctis addressed them with a dreamy gaze, "Greetings, travellers. The tapestry of Somnia's dreams is fraying, and we beseech your aid in restoring its enchantment."

As they explored Somnia's fantastical landscapes, they encountered Fantasy Spirits ethereal beings that embodied the essence of imagination and dreams. Each Fantasy Spirit held a different aspect of Somnia's creative tapestry.

Scarlette marvelled, "It's like stepping into a world of ever-shifting stories."

Marcus noted, "And every choice we make becomes a chapter in Somnia's boundless tale."

Alex affirmed, "Our role is to rekindle the realm's creative spirit and restore its imaginative balance."

Guided by the Dreamweavers, they faced dream-themed puzzles that required their understanding of fantasy, symbolism, and creative interpretation. They crafted narratives, unlocked allegorical gates, and embraced the whimsy of imagination, aiming to restore Somnia's fantastical equilibrium.

Dreamweaver Noctis praised their dedication, "Your actions are like inkwells that replenish Somnia's quill."

By embracing their sense of wonder and collaborating with the Fantasy Spirits, they sought to mend the unravelling threads of imagination and rejuvenate the realm's creative essence. They confronted the Dreambound Abyss a rift of forgotten dreams and through their combined imaginative effort, they restored its wondrous equilibrium.

Dreamweaver Noctis expressed gratitude, "You are weavers of dreams, and your actions have rekindled Somnia's stories."

With the Dreambound Abyss sealed, Somnia's landscapes once again shifted with ever-shifting tales. Every step was a new adventure, and the realm resonated with the magic of creative possibility.

Dreamweaver Noctis offered tokens of appreciation, "As symbols of our gratitude, we present you with Fable Stones—stones that capture the essence of Somnia's stories."

Fable Stones possessed the power to manipulate and project imaginative constructs within limits, conjuring fantastical scenarios, unravelling symbolic mysteries, and even connecting with the essence of the narrative. They were a testament to the trio's role in preserving Somnia's imaginative equilibrium.

As they left Somnia, Dippy's voice echoed from the D-Phone.

"Somnia's stories are richer due to your imaginative interventions.

Your journey continues to shape the dimensions."

With Fable Stones in their possession and a sense of accomplishment warming their hearts, the trio once again faced the array of trains. Each train beckoned with the promise of new adventures, opportunities to learn, and chances to contribute to the dimensions they visited.

Amid the enchanting landscapes of Esmeira, Alex, Marcus, and Scarlette found themselves wandering through the enchanting realm of Esmeira once again, their laughter and excitement filling the air.

As they explored the vibrant streets lined with peculiar shops and fantastical creatures, their stomachs began to rumble. "I'm starving!" Marcus exclaimed, his hand resting on his growling belly.

"Agreed. All this dimension-hopping sure works up an appetite," Scarlette added, her eyes scanning the bustling surroundings.

Just then, a tantalising aroma wafted through the air, capturing their attention. Following their noses, they stumbled upon a colourful Esmeiran fast-food place named "Flavour Fusion Delights,"

a symphony of tantalising aromas enveloped them. The air was filled with a medley of scents that seemed to dance and weave around their senses, promising an extraordinary culinary experience. Their gazes were immediately drawn to the intricate decorations that adorned every corner of the restaurant, a visual feast of hues that seemed to radiate a magical aura.

A cheerful bell chimed as they entered, and their eyes widened in amazement as they scanned the menu. It was as if the menu itself was a work of art, each dish described with poetic detail that made their mouths water.

And to their astonishment, they saw their favourite items listed: "Portal Cakes, Glittering Gobstoppers, Sparkling Nectar Fries, Jewel Candy Sundaes, and Strawberry Brew Floats."

"Whoa, this is like a dream come true!"

Alex exclaimed, unable to contain his excitement.

Scarlette's eyes sparkled with wonder.

"I can't believe it! It's like they've combined all our favourite treats into one place."

As they placed their orders, a sassy and vibrant woman with multi-coloured hair approached their table.

"Hey there, newcomers! Welcome to Flavour Fusion Delights.

Name's Butterscotch, and I'm the proud owner of this little slice of Esmeiran heaven."

Butterscotch's energy matched the lively atmosphere of the place. She explained, "Here in Esmeira, we use a special currency called ghost coins for transactions. But since it's your first time here and I can see you're a bunch of food enthusiasts, consider your first meal on the house!"

Their gratitude was evident in their expressions as they thanked Butterscotch.

The food arrived in a spectacular burst of colours and textures that looked almost surreal, like art on a plate. As they took their first bites, their eyes widened with surprise. The flavours were more vibrant, the aromas more intoxicating, and the tastes more intense than anything they had ever experienced.

"These Sparkling Nectar Fries are on a whole other level!" Marcus declared, his taste buds overwhelmed by the explosion of flavours.

Scarlette's laughter tinkled like wind chimes as she savoured her Jewel Candy Sundae.

"It's like I've stepped into a fairy tale where every bite is pure magic."

Alex nodded in agreement, his eyes shining as he took a bite of the Glittering Gobstopper. "And these flavours... they're so rich and complex. It's like they've taken our beloved treats and amplified them a hundredfold."

Even the Strawberry Brew Float, a familiar favourite, tasted entirely new in this enchanting realm. The strawberry flavours burst forth like a cascade of sweet and tart notes, each sip an adventure in itself.

As they indulged in their sumptuous feast, the restaurant seemed to come alive with a special energy, as if the food itself was imbued with the essence of Esmeira. Each bite transported them further into a world of delight and wonder, a place where their senses were heightened and their taste buds rejoiced.

Amid their laughter and joyful chatter, they couldn't help but appreciate the way the flavours resonated with the vibrant ambience of the restaurant. It was as if every dish told a story, and with each bite, they were uncovering a new chapter of Esmeira's culinary magic.

As they finished their meal, sated and exhilarated, Butterscotch approached their table once more, a mischievous glint in her eye. "So, how was your first taste of Esmeira?"

Alex grinned, leaning back in his seat. "Honestly, it's like we've never really tasted food before."

Butterscotch laughed, her laughter carrying the warmth of hospitality.

"Esmeira has a way of making the ordinary extraordinary. And if you're ready for more, you know where to find me."

With a friendly wink, Butterscotch left them to soak in the enchantment of their meal. As they sat there, their hearts and stomachs full, they couldn't help but anticipate the adventure that awaited them in this realm of endless surprises and boundless flavours.

Suddenly, Dippy call their attention "Ahem, excuse me, mortals." Dippy's voice sounded from the D-Phone.

"As much as I hate to interrupt your culinary enjoyment, I have some urgent news to deliver."

The trio exchanged a curious glance before focusing their attention on the D-Phone.

"What's going on, Dippy?" Alex asked.

"In the Dimension of Ludicrous Legumes, trouble is brewing," Dippy informed them with a solemn tone.

"The balance of that realm is under threat, and I sense that the Sceptre might be connected to this."

Scarlette's eyes sparkled with intrigue. "Could this be the clue we've been waiting for?"

"Seems like it," Alex replied. "All right, we're on it. How do we get there?"

"Get ready for an adventure, my friends," Dippy replied. "To enter the Dimension of Ludicrous Legumes, you'll need to ride the Whirlwind Roller Coaster, located just a few blocks away from Flavour Fusion Delights."

"More Roller Coasters?" Marcus grumbled with his stomach full "Oh man, this isn't going to go down well"

"Just watch out for Snake legs" Alex said concerned whilst looking out the window and they all briefly hid underneath the table as they spotted the creature slither by as it had already stolen food off a disgruntled customer after biting him, leaving him temporarily frozen. "It Ssssure tastes goood!" the creature taunted whilst eating his food and then it disappeared off site.

With their meal finished and excitement building anew, the trio dashed out of the restaurant, following the directions to the Whirlwind Roller Coaster.

As they approached the towering structure, they couldn't help but be awed by its intricate design, a mix of magical architecture and mechanical wonder.

With a mixture of anticipation and nerves, they took their seats in the roller coaster vibrant trains, and as the ride began, they were hurled into a whirlwind of twists, turns, and loops that defied the laws of physics. The wind whistled past their ears, and their screams of exhilaration mixed with laughter as they zoomed through portals that seemed to bridge dimensions.

After what felt like both a thrilling instant and an eternity, the roller coaster came to a stop, and they found themselves amid a whimsical landscape. Fields of oversized vegetables and peculiar plants stretched before them, and the scent of fresh earth filled the air.

"This is it," Alex said, his excitement palpable. "The Dimension of Ludicrous Legumes."

As they prepared to embark on their mission to uncover the truth behind the Sceptre and restore balance to this dimension, they knew that their journey was just beginning, and the challenges ahead would test their courage, resourcefulness, and friendship in ways they had never imagined.

CHAPTER FOUR

LAUGHTER'S ECHO IN LUDICROUS LEGUMES

"So here we are!" Dippy's synthetic voice echoed through the air as Alex and his companions disembarked from a roller coaster train adorned with fantastical vegetables that seemed to defy the laws of nature.

The platform itself exuded an otherworldly charm, with vines of rainbow-coloured ivy winding around its edges.

The train station was a symphony of colours and shapes, reminiscent of a surreal artist's palette.

They had arrived in the whimsically named "Dimension of Ludicrous Legumes."

The transition had been unlike anything they had experienced before.

As they stepped onto the platform, the air around them shimmered with an otherworldly energy.

The atmosphere was tinged with a sweet aroma that seemed to blend the scents of freshly baked bread and blooming flowers.

"Alex and his friends exchanged intrigued glances, excitement bubbling within them.

The platform itself was unlike any train station they had seen, adorned with cascades of climbing vines that were intertwined with oversized beans and kale leaves.

The sky overhead was a mesmerising blend of vibrant hues shades of green and orange danced harmoniously, casting an ethereal glow across the landscape.

"I must admit, Ludicrous Legumes seems like a place straight out of a dream," Marcus mused, his eyes wide with wonder.

"Agreed," Scarlette chimed in, a grin tugging at the corner of her lips.

With a sense of wonder and determination, Alex, Scarlette, and Marcus stepped into the Dimension of Ludicrous Legumes.

The ground beneath their feet felt springy like they were walking on cushions made of moss and leaves. The sky above them seemed to be a perpetual blend of sunrise and sunset, casting a warm and ethereal glow over the landscape.

The three friends couldn't help but marvel at the bizarre flora that surrounded them. Trees with leaves that resembled spinning tops, mushrooms that twinkled like stars, and vines that emitted musical notes when touched Ludicrous Legumes was a realm of whimsy and magic that defied all logic.

"Wow," Marcus breathed, his eyes wide as he took in the surreal beauty of their surroundings. "This place is like something out of a fantastical dream."

"Indeed," Scarlette agreed, her voice filled with awe. "I've never seen anything like this before."

"But we're not here just to admire the scenery," Alex reminded them, his tone serious.

"Dippy mentioned chaos and a missing artefact. We need to find out what's going on and if the sceptre is here."

As they began to explore the vibrant landscape, they noticed that the air was filled with a faint hum, like an undercurrent of energy. Following the sound, they soon stumbled upon a clearing where a group of peculiar creatures were gathered.

These creatures, known as Flibberbeans, resembled a cross between bouncy beans and mischievous pixies. They bounced and tumbled around, leaving trails of sparkling dust in their wake.

Approaching cautiously, Alex cleared his throat to get their attention. "Excuse me, we're travellers from another dimension. We've heard that there might be some trouble here. Can you tell us what's going on?"

The Flibberbeans stopped their antics and turned to look at the newcomers with wide eyes and curious expressions.

One of them, who seemed to be the leader with a golden crown made of leaves, stepped forward. We don't know what you are talking about as you can see, we are fine and joyful. As soon as they left the enchanting experience with the Flibberbeans in the hidden glade, Scarlette, Marcus and Alex's excitement were momentarily dampened by a feeling of annoyance.

As they left the glade, they exchanged glances that conveyed their frustration with Dippy's earlier false information about finding the sceptre.

Upon leaving the glade, they found themselves in a small clearing, where the sunlight streamed through the canopy of trees. The air was filled with a gentle breeze that carried with it a sense of renewal. Scarlette's irritation began to dissipate, replaced by a renewed determination to continue their adventure.

As they walked through the Enchanted Woodlands, Scarlette and Alex discussed their next steps.

"We can't let Dippy's misinformation ruin the magic of this journey," Alex remarked.

"We've come this far, and we still have the Ludicrous Legumes. Who knows what they might hold?"

Scarlette nodded in agreement. "You're right. Let's focus on the positive experiences we've gained, the friendships we've made, and the lessons we've learned.

And who knows, maybe there's more to the story of the sceptre that we're yet to uncover."

Their spirits lifted, and Scarlette and Alex continued their journey through the woodlands.

Along the way, they encountered a playful group of forest sprites who guided them through a series of riddles and challenges, each designed to test their creativity, wit, and ability to work together.

After successfully completing these challenges, the sprites led them to a serene waterfall, where they could rest and reflect.

Scarlette dipped her hand into the cool water, lost in thought.

"You know, Alex, even though we didn't find the sceptre as we expected, this journey has been so much more than we could have imagined."

Alex smiled, gazing at the shimmering water. "Absolutely. We've grown, learned, and expanded our horizons.

And who's to say the sceptre isn't waiting for us at the end of another adventure?"

As they continued their conversation, a soft voice interrupted them. It was Dippy, his holographic form appearing beside them.

"I apologise for the confusion earlier," Dippy began.

"I realise my mistake in misleading you about the sceptre.

I understand your annoyance, but I hope you can see the value in the experiences you've gained."

Scarlette sighed, her annoyance softening. "Dippy, it's not just about finding artefacts or magical items. It's about the journey itself, the people we meet, and the stories we create along the way."

Dippy nodded. "You're right. And to make amends for my error, I have a new task for you one that could reward you with Silver a Ghost Coin."

Scarlette, Marcus and Alex exchanged curious glances, intrigued by the new task.

"But let's not forget our mission, shall we?

What's the task we need to complete to earn those Silver Ghost coins, Dippy?"

Dippy's holographic screen flickered to life, displaying the task that awaited them:

"You must Make the ruler of this dimension, King Jabez, laugh to earn 400 Silver Ghost Coins."

"Making him laugh?" might be trickier than it sounds,"

Alex pondered aloud, gazing at the peculiar environment around them.

"The Dimension of Ludicrous Legumes," Dippy declared, the words carrying a sense of anticipation.

"Ludicrous Legumes," Alex chuckled, his voice tinged with amusement. "Well, no matter the name, we've got a mission to accomplish

"The challenge is to make the ruler of this dimension, King Jabez, genuinely laugh," Dippy explained, its digital voice conveying a mix of instruction and intrigue. "If you succeed, you'll be rewarded with 400 Silver Ghost Coins."

"Make him laugh?" Scarlette's eyes narrowed, her curiosity piqued. "That's... an interesting task."

"We could try telling him jokes," Marcus suggested with a shrug.

"But I doubt it's that straightforward," Alex mused, his brow furrowed in thought.

"Indeed," Dippy affirmed. "The real challenge lies in engaging in an insult-hurling match with King Jabez. If your humour cracks his facade, the coins are yours."

"And if we fail?" Scarlette inquired, her gaze fixed on Dippy.

"We return empty-handed," Alex replied with a nonchalant shrug.

"Or perhaps not," Dippy added with a hint of disdain.

"There might be more at stake than we realise."

"What do you mean, Dippy?" Alex's voice was laced with curiosity as he held the D-Phone close.

"Watch." The D-Phone's screen flickered and a scene unfolded before them.

King Jabez was seated on his throne and three of his weird vegetable subjects stood before him. Each had a go at hurling insults at the king. Each failed to make him laugh. The King shook his head and pressed a button on the armrest of his throne. A trapdoor slid open and the three subjects fell down the deep chasm. The view moved to show them down there, being eaten alive by a huge carnivorous plant resembling a Venus Fly Trap.

"Good heavens!" Marcus and Scarlette cried together. "That's absolutely bonkers."

"That could happen to us if we can't make the King laugh." Alex nodded. "But I'm confident that we can do this. Vesta said I am destined for greatness."

"And why would you believe her?" Scarlette raised an eyebrow.

"She's... an overseer of the worlds," Alex replied with a smirk. "Now come on."

With the ancient golden leather book called "Guide to Worlds",

Alex's supernatural energy transported them into King Jabez's throne room.

The King looked up at them startled and then gave them a wide grin.

With determination coursing through their veins, the trio strode into the heart of King Jabez's palace, the grandeur of the room magnifying the weight of their mission.

"Salutations, King Jabez," Alex addressed the ruler, a courteous nod accompanying his words.

"We're here to embrace your challenge."

"So, you are here to win the prize." He said.

"Yes, we are." Alex grinned back.

"Alright then." The king nodded.

The air hummed with energy, an unspoken challenge between Alex and the vegetable King taking shape.

The King's eyes gleamed with a playful spark as he reclined on his throne.

"Ah, the brave challengers. Let the contest of wit commence!"

"Let us begin."

And so, the verbal duel began. King Jabez and Alex hurled insults, their words echoing through the chamber in a lively exchange.

But this was no ordinary exchange their insults flowed in a whimsical rhythm, their banter becoming a battle of rhyming retorts.

"Your laughter shall be but a fleeting breeze,

While I unravel your pomp with perfect ease," Alex quipped with a grin.

The King countered, his voice dripping with sly amusement,

"*Oh, young traveller, with your aim so high,*

Yet your words falter, reaching only the sky."

The energy in the room intensified with each exchange, the audience of peculiar vegetables observing with a mix of intrigue and amusement. As the duel continued, a mischievous glint sparkled in Alex's eyes.

"*King Jabez, your crown may gleam with gold,*

But your jokes are as stale as stories old."

Laughter echoed through the chamber, as the King responded in kind,

"*Your retorts may be sharp, but it's clear to see,*
In this realm of humour, you can't beat me."

The atmosphere vibrated with tension and mirth, the repartee growing sharper and more imaginative with every turn.

The rhymes continued to flow, a spirited contest between wit and charm.

With the insult match drawing to a close, the battle of words reached its zenith.

A few minutes later, the King pretended to laugh.

Laughter erupted from King Jabez, a sound that reverberated through the grand chamber. The King's amusement and the trio exchanged glances.

"We did it!" Alex clapped his hands.

"No, we didn't." Scarlette whispered shaking her head.

"That's the fakest laugh ever, and he's pressing on that trapdoor button."

The floor beneath them gave way with a jolt, plunging Alex and his two best friends into an abyss of darkness.

The rush of air whistled past their ears as they descended, their hearts pounding with a mix of terror and anticipation.

Their descent seemed endless, a dizzying spiral into the depths of the unknown, right toward the waiting tentacles and jaws of the carnivorous plant.

Finally, with a bone-rattling crash, they landed in a dimly lit chamber, surrounded by jagged rock formations. The echoes of their impact reverberated through the space, and before they could regain their bearings, the ominous silhouette of the carnivorous plant materialised before them.

Its tentacles quivered with excitement, its gaping maw poised to devour its unexpected visitors.

"Don't worry; I'm getting us out of here," Alex declared with determination, his voice cutting through the tense silence.

He leapt to his feet, his fingers snapping in a practiced rhythm, channelling the supernatural energy that had aided them on their journey.

But this time, his fingers met resistance, the magic flickering like a dying ember.

Frantic energy coursed through Alex's veins as he continued to snap his fingers, his brow furrowed in concentration. Yet, nothing happened. The dark dungeon remained unchanged, and the carnivorous plant inched ever closer, its tendrils reaching out like greedy claws.

Scarlette's eyes widened with a mixture of fear and frustration.

"What's happening? Why isn't it working?"

"The magic powers I have..." Alex's voice trailed off, his frustration palpable.

"It's not working down here."

"Or maybe you've exhausted your powers," Marcus suggested, his voice steady despite the dire circumstances.

Desperation etched on their faces, the trio backed against the cold, rocky wall as the carnivorous plant loomed closer, its ravenous hunger evident in its every movement.

"So, we're going to be eaten alive?" Scarlette screamed.

"We can't give up," Alex growled, his eyes flashing with determination.

"We need to find another way

"Not necessarily," Dippy replied. "You can use the Holographic Sword."

"What's that?" The three of them asked together.

The D-Phone activated the app that made a long sword made of laser light eject from it.

"It can cut through anything."

"Dippy." Alex sighed and held the sword before him. "I do wish you'd not wait for the last moment to tell us these things."

"I save my energy until it's necessary," Dippy said with a snort.

A long sword formed before them, its blade crafted from vibrant laser light that glinted with otherworldly energy.

With newfound hope, Alex seized the Holographic Sword, its weight and balance feeling surprisingly natural in his grip.

The blade hummed with power, a tangible extension of his resolve.

Without a moment's hesitation, he charged at the carnivorous plant, the sword's radiant edge slicing through the air with a resolute swish.

The battle was fierce, a symphony of clashing metal and snapping jaws. The carnivorous plant retaliated with its tentacles, lashing out with deadly precision.

Scarlette and Marcus stood at Alex's side, their weapons drawn, fighting back the encroaching tendrils.

As they battled, the chamber seemed to shift around them, revealing the presence of intricate mechanisms and devices hidden within the rocky walls.

Pressure plates triggered spears that shot from the walls, pendulum blades swung menacingly, and hidden pitfalls threatened to swallow them whole.

The room had become a treacherous puzzle, a deadly dance of survival against the carnivorous plant's defences.

With a triumphant cry, Alex's sword cleaved through a particularly thick tentacle, causing the plant to shriek in agony.

As the plant recoiled, Marcus spotted a series of pressure-sensitive tiles on the ground. "Step lightly!"

The trio navigated the shifting landscape with precision, their movements synchronised as they evaded the deadly traps. With every strike, the Holographic Sword carved a path of safety through the perilous chamber.

And then, with one final swing, Alex severed the last of the carnivorous plant's tendrils, leaving it defeated and crumbling.

The chamber shuddered, the echoes of their victory mingling with the rumble of collapsing rock. Above them, King Jabez's voice rose in a screech of dismay.

"My pet!" King Jabez screeched from above. "What have you done?"

"And we'll do that to all your pets…" Alex retorted defiantly, his eyes ablaze with determination. "If you don't give us a fair chance to win the ghost coins."

"All right then come on up and make me laugh," Jabez said with a deep sigh.

The second round of insults began.

The challenge remained unresolved, but victory was theirs at that moment. They had conquered the carnivorous plant and emerged from the perilous chamber stronger and more united than ever before. With the Holographic Sword's radiant light still gleaming, they turned their attention upward, ready to face whatever lay ahead in their pursuit of the elusive Silver Ghost coins.

The atmosphere in the throne room crackled with tension as King Jabez and Alex engaged in a battle of words.

Their insults, sharp as thorns, flew back and forth in a verbal duel that echoed through the chamber. Each retort was a carefully crafted rhyme, designed to provoke a reaction from the other.

King Jabez, with a sly grin, fired the first shot:

"Your wit's as dull as a butter knife,

Your words lack punch, it's plain to see.

A challenger bold, but in this fight,

You're but a pebble in the vast sea."

Alex didn't flinch, his resolve unyielding:

"Your laughter's forced, a hollow sound,

A ruler wrapped in arrogance's shroud.

Your ego swells, your wisdom's bound,

In this contest of words, you're not allowed."

The room seemed to hold its breath as the exchange intensified, with Scarlette and Marcus watching the duel with bated breath.

As the battle raged on, the insults became more creative and daring:

King Jabez grinned, his eyes glinting:

"Your jokes fall flat, like old deflated tires,

Your attempts at humour, mere embers glows.

A challenger dauntless, but your insults are dire,

In this war of wits, you're merely a shadow."

Alex's retort was swift and biting:

"Your demeanour's cold, like a frosty night,

Your laughter's fake, a façade of glee.

A ruler aloof, lost in his own might,

In this battlefield of banter, I hold the key."

As the insults continued, the very air seemed to vibrate with the intensity of their words. The room was electrified with energy; each rhymes a stroke in a masterpiece of linguistic combat.

King Jabez unleashed a barrage of retorts that left Alex momentarily flustered:

"Your jokes are stale, like week-old bread,

Your words are weak, they lack the punch.

A challenger fierce, but in this thread,

You're but a whisper, a passing hunch."

Yet, Alex's determination shone through, his next words ringing with conviction:

"Your laughter's hollow, like an empty gourd,

Your jests are feeble; they miss the mark.

A ruler aloof, with a fake reward,

In this clash of minds, you've missed the spark."

And then, as if the universe itself held its breath, King Jabez let out a genuine burst of laughter, his eyes crinkling with mirth. The tension in the room dissipated like mist, replaced by a palpable sense of camaraderie.

The King's hearty laughter reverberated through the chamber, a symphony of victory that resonated with Alex and his friends.

"We did it," Alex grinned at his companions. "This time, we've earned the four hundred silver ghost coins."

With the challenge conquered and the reward secured, Alex was presented with a large Silver Ghost Coin, a shimmering token of their triumph.

The King also conjured a shower of smaller Silver Ghost coins that cascaded like rain, a gesture of goodwill. Alex grinned as he caught a handful of coins, sharing them with Scarlette and Marcus and he pocketed a Large Silver Ghost "Power" coin that had an engraving of a generic ghost.

As they stepped out of the Dimension of Ludicrous Legumes, the group carried with them not only their hard-won reward but also the memories of their daring escapades in the peculiar realm. The portal back home swirled into existence before them, a shimmering gateway that led them back to their familiar world.

"Another adventure down," Alex mused, his thoughts echoing in the minds of his companions.

"Indeed," Scarlette grinned, her eyes glinting with excitement.

"And it's not every day you get to engage in an insult contest with a vegetable king and face down a carnivorous plant."

"I still can't believe you pulled out that laser sword thing," Marcus chuckled, shaking his head in amazement.

"Talk about saving the best for last."

"Dippy, always full of surprises," Alex winked at the D-Phone, which emitted a satisfied electronic beep.

"Well, I do aim to keep things interesting," Dippy chimed.

As they stepped through the portal, Moments later, they found themselves back in their world, standing near the portal platform they had originally used to access the Dimension of Legumes.

"This time, the four hundred silver ghost coins are ours!" Scarlette declared with a satisfied smile.

"Now, let's go and revel in our victory," Marcus shouted with excitement, his applause punctuating the moment.

As the chamber doors swung open, Alex, Scarlette, and Marcus stepped out, the echoes of their adventure still reverberating in their hearts.

"Now, let's head out and buy those extravagant D Blasters!," Marcus chimed in excitedly, his hands clapping together.

CHAPTER FIVE

"FLIGHT AMONG THE AVIAN SOCIETY"

"We got the D-blasters!" Marcus said happily, holding his weapon close to his chest.

"And the E-Jet packs! "Scarlette beamed as the three of them stepped out of the colourful shop. The Esmeria Jet packs or "E-Jet packs" resembled motorcycles with no wheels but they were Jet packs that boosted you through the air once you switched on the gear.

"And now what do we do?" Marcus wondered leaving the shop, as the sun cast a warm golden glow over the lush landscape of Esmeria, Alex and his friends decided to soar through the sky on their E-Jet Packs.

The wind whistled past their ears as they revelled in the exhilarating sensation of flight. They performed loops, twists, and daring dives, each maneuver filling them with a sense of freedom and adventure.

As they zipped through the sky, the vibrant colours of Esmeria's landscape unfolded beneath them like a living painting.

Emerald-green forests, sparkling rivers, and majestic mountains stretched out in all directions, forming a breath-taking panorama that captivated their senses.

Eventually, the friends decided to venture into the heart of the forest.

The dense canopy of trees enveloped them, providing a cool shade that contrasted with the warmth of the open skies.

The forest was teeming with life, from colourful birds that matched the hues of the landscape to exotic flora that seemed to emit a soft, enchanting glow.

Alex, always curious, led the group deeper into the forest, their jetpacks humming softly as they glided between the towering trees.

The air was filled with the soothing sounds of nature, a symphony of chirping insects and rustling leaves. After a while, they came upon a clearing, and their attention was immediately drawn to a sight that left them awestruck.

Before them stood a collection of intricately designed structures, a harmonious blend of nature and architecture. These buildings were unlike anything they had ever seen, resembling giant nests woven from iridescent materials, their surfaces reflecting the colours of the surroundings.

Bridges and walkways connected the structures, creating a network that seemed to float effortlessly among the treetops.

As they cautiously approached, they noticed figures moving about the structures. These humanoid creatures had avian features, with feathered bodies, wings, and elegant beaks.

Each detail of their appearance was a testament to the delicate balance between nature and artistry.

The creatures seemed to notice the newcomers, their gazes turning toward Alex and his friends. Despite their initial surprise, the avian beings did not display any signs of hostility. Instead, a sense of curiosity emanated from their eyes as they observed the humans and their unfamiliar technology.

Alex, drawn by both his adventurous spirit and his desire to learn, approached one of the avian beings who appeared to be the leader of this extraordinary society.

With gestures and a few simple words that transcended language barriers, he conveyed his fascination and respect for their way of life.

The avian leader, known as Avaela, responded with a mixture of trills and melodious tones. Through a combination of gestures and their form of communication, Avaela shared the story of their society—a society that had existed for generations, founded on the principles of harmony with nature, artistry, and a deep connection to the land.

The society lived in harmony with the forest, utilising its resources with utmost care and reverence. Their nests were constructed using naturally sourced materials, and their artistic expressions were woven into the very fabric of their daily lives. Music, dance, and storytelling were integral parts of their culture, serving to bind their community together and strengthen their bonds.

Alex and his friends were invited to explore their society, to witness their artistic rituals and immerse themselves in their way of life.

They were taught the basics of their unique form of communication, allowing for a deeper connection despite their differences.

Dippy, had been more than eager to share fascinating details about the advanced society of the humanoid bird creatures.

He animatedly described how they had managed to strike a harmonious balance with nature, their unique communication methods, and their intricate nests that seemed to meld seamlessly with the surrounding forest.

It was during this conversation that Dippy had mentioned rumours of a powerful artefact, a magical sceptre, which was believed to hold significance in the avian society.

As the sun began to dip below the horizon, casting a warm orange glow across the treetops, Scarlette's unease became evident as she cautioned her friends about the potential risks of delving deeper into the avian society, pointing out subtle warning signs that others might have missed.

Despite her warnings, the glint of determination in Alex's eyes was hard to ignore.

He believed that the magic sceptre could be the key to understanding the avian society on a profound level, a bridge between their world and this enchanting dimension and it could be the sceptre that they are looking for!

Hovering on their E-Jet Packs amidst the towering trees, Marcus and Scarlette exchanged concerned glances as Alex's excitement seemed to override his usual sense of caution.

With a hand signal, Alex indicated that he had spotted the magic sceptre, situated next to one of the slumbering chief birds. He planned to retrieve it stealthily, allowing them to examine it without disrupting the tranquillity of the moment.

Scarlette's voice, a whisper laden with anxiety, reached Alex's ears.

"Alex, I really think this is a bad idea. There's something about this situation that doesn't sit right."

But determination had wrapped its tendrils around Alex's mind, and he was willing to take the risk.

Gently manoeuvring his E-Jet Pack, he glided toward the sleeping chief bird, his heart pounding in his chest.

His friends held their breath, eyes locked on his every move. Inching closer, his fingertips almost brushing the magic sceptre, Alex's movements became more cautious, his breath shallow. It was then that a comically timed mishap occurred.

As if, guided by some mischievous spirit of chaos, a stray leaf detached from a nearby branch and fluttered down, landing gently on the chief bird's beak.

The effect was instantaneous, the chief bird jerked awake, squawking in alarm. In a swift motion, it reached out and grasped the magic sceptre, a jolt of urgency igniting its senses.

A series of loud squawks reverberated through the forest as the chief bird sounded the alarm, rousing its fellow avian beings from their slumber.

Alex's heart raced as panic washed over him. Without a second thought, he lunged forward and snatched the sceptre from the chief bird's grasp.

The avian chief's call grew louder, its shrill cries echoing through the trees. During the chaos, Alex activated his E-Jet Pack and soared into the air, his friends following suit.

However, their attempt at a swift retreat was met with unexpected challenges. The avian creatures, awakened and alerted, had taken to the skies in pursuit. With winged determination, they streaked through the air, their agile forms slicing through the currents as they attempted to reclaim the stolen sceptre.

In a bid to evade their relentless pursuers, Alex tossed the sceptre to Marcus, who caught it with a mix of awe and surprise.

As they flew, the gang played a nerve-wracking game of keep-away, tossing the sceptre between them as the avian creatures swooped and darted, their claws grazing the air just inches away from their prize.

Amidst the chaos, Alex's grip on his E-Jet Pack faltered, and with a heart-stopping jolt, he was sent hurtling downward. He crashed into the ground with a thud, his E-Jet Pack spiralling out of control before steadying itself.

Scarlet and Marcus cried out in alarm, their voices a mix of concern and urgency.

With a groan, Alex pushed himself up from the ground, his determination stronger than ever. He reactivated his E-Jet Pack and re-joined the fray, just as Marcus tossed the sceptre back to him. With the avian creatures closing in, Alex made a split-second decision he flung the sceptre high into the air.

As it soared upward, the friends followed its trajectory, their eyes wide with anticipation.

The sceptre seemed to hang in the air for a suspended moment before gravity began to claim it once more. Acting on instinct, Alex lunged forward, his fingers barely grazing the artefact before he was sent tumbling back.

The sceptre, however, was captured mid-air by Scarlette, who held it aloft triumphantly.

With the magic sceptre secure in their possession, Alex, Scarlette, and Marcus made a hasty retreat, their E-Jet Packs propelling them through the sky with urgency. The avian creatures pursued them relentlessly, their wings slicing through the air as they attempted to intercept the fleeing humans.

The situation grew increasingly perilous as the avian creatures closed in, their determination undeterred. In a daring maneuver, Alex tossed the sceptre to Marcus, who deftly caught it while Scarlette engaged in evasive maneuvers to confuse their pursuers.

But in the midst of the chaos, a particularly agile avian creature managed to seize the sceptre from Marcus' grasp.

With a shout of dismay, Alex lunged forward, reaching out in a final attempt to reclaim the artefact but it was too late the avian creature, clutching the sceptre, veered away and rejoined its fellow pursuers, triumphant cries echoing through the air.

Desperation etched into his expression, Alex watched as the avian creatures faded into the distance, the stolen sceptre held high among them. As his friends circled back to join him, concern etched on their faces, Alex couldn't help but feel a mixture of frustration and determination.

"We might have lost the sceptre for now," he said, his voice tinged with a fierce resolve,

"but we'll find a way to get it back. We've glimpsed their world, their society, and now we have a purpose, a purpose that's bigger than ever before."

As Alex shook off the remnants of his dizziness, he noticed a sudden change in the atmosphere around them. A feeling of tension hung in the air, like a storm brewing on the horizon.

Looking up, his gaze was met by an unexpected sight, the sky above was filled with figures descending from the clouds, their forms majestic and imposing.

These were the Guardians of Vesta, ethereal beings who radiated an aura of power and authority. With wings outstretched, they landed gracefully around Alex and his friends, forming a protective circle. Their eyes, a brilliant shade of iridescent blue, locked onto the avian creatures who had pursued them.

During the confrontation, a presence more commanding than the rest descended from the heavens. Vesta herself, the Overseer of Esmeira, appeared before them, her presence both awe-inspiring and comforting. Her gown seemed to shimmer with the very essence of the cosmos, and her eyes held a depth of knowledge that transcended mortal comprehension.

"What is the meaning of this disturbance?"

Vesta's voice held a regal authority, and her gaze shifted from the avian creatures to the humans and back again.

The chief bird stepped forward, its feathers ruffling with a mix of apprehension and indignation. In a series of trills and squawks, it recounted the events, accusing Alex and his friends of trespassing and theft.

Alex's voice rose, his tone firm and resolute.

"Hold on a minute! We're not thieves.

We stumbled upon your society by accident, and we thought you had taken our magic sceptre." The avian creatures erupted in a chorus of disbelieving squawks. As Alex's words settled in, they exchanged confused glances before one of them approached the chief bird and whispered urgently.

With a startled realisation, the chief bird turned back to Alex, its demeanour shifting from accusatory to understanding.

It gestured toward a pedestal, upon which rested another sceptre their own sceptre, which they had been guarding and now saw in Alex's possession.

A moment of realisation passed between the humans and the avian creatures, the gravity of the misunderstanding settling in.

Scarlette's hand went to her forehead in disbelief, and Marcus let out a sheepish laugh.

Alex stepped forward, the truth weighing heavily on him.

"I apologise for our mistake. We never meant to take your sceptre. It was an accident."

The chief bird let out a low, grumbling squawk before turning back to Vesta. With a gesture of its wing, it indicated that punishment should be meted out for the trespass.

But Vesta's voice cut through the tension, firm and unwavering.

"No harm shall come to these visitors."

The avian creatures grunted and voiced their disapproval, but they yielded to Vesta's authority. With a final glare at Alex and his friends, they retreated to their society, leaving the humans and Guardians behind.

Vesta's gaze softened as she turned her attention back to Alex and his friends.

"You have shown bravery in the face of adversity but remember that meddling in forbidden territories can have grave consequences.

There is wisdom in curiosity, but it must be tempered with caution."

She extended her hand, a radiant energy swirling within her palm.

"For your bravery, I offer you these Little Silver Ghost Coins.

Use them wisely"

Alex and his friends accepted the coins with grateful smiles, humbled by Vesta's words.

As quickly as she had appeared, the Queen of Esmeira faded from view, her presence leaving behind a sense of wonder and awe.

With a renewed sense of purpose and a newfound appreciation for the importance of caution, Alex and his friends activated their E-Jet Packs, soaring through the sky once more.

The forest and its enigmatic inhabitants retreated beneath them, and the world of Esmeira embraced them with its boundless beauty.

As they looked back at the forest, Alex spotted a bar, "Look, that looks like a bar." Alex pointed at the dining zone that served fast food. "Let's get a bite to eat before going back home. I'm starving."

The bright and cosy bar was nothing like what they had back home. They ordered the huge Super Burgers, the giant Donuts filled with Peanut Butter and Jam, Gooey Gummy Snakes and tall glasses of delicious Strawberry Brew. All that cost them just three Ghost Coins.

As they enjoyed their food, Alex noticed a tall figure walk into the bar. He was hunched and kept looking over his shoulder from time to time as he ordered his meal. Alex kept an eye on the mysterious man, and when the hooded man turned to look Alex's way, his yellow eyes blinked. The man took his order from the counter and walked up to the seat next to the three.

"Who are you, mister?" Alex whispered to the hooded man. "Are you hiding from the law?"

"None of your business" The man almost snarled and then lowered his tone. "Pardon me, young man. I'm... I..."

"Are you in some kind of trouble?" Scarlette leaned over to ask.

"I'm being hunted, by an evil dictator." The hooded man said in a low whisper. "He wanted me to kill my own friend, but I refused... so he wants to kill me now."

"What is your name?" Alex peered at the man.

With a deep sigh, he pulled his hood back and said. "I am Ruok. I come from the Thunder Forest World dimension. The Dictator, Vezan, from my world, wants me dead."

"Good heavens." Scarlette shook a little at Ruok's very wild appearance. He wild hair nearly covering all of his face and he wore sheepskin. He looked like a caveman and looked a little bewildered.

"Aw, come on, Scarlette." Alex laughed. "We've seen all sorts of crazy things in the last few hours than we have ever seen before in our lives"

"Is he like a caveman?" Marcus asked before sinking his teeth into a large and tender super burger.

"I don't think so." Alex laughed. "He's just what he is. So Ruok, where are you going to hide?"

119

"I'm hopping from dimension to dimension now." Ruok said with a shake of his head. "Keeping a step ahead of Vezan's cruel hunters. I have powers beyond your imagination that is helping me do this."

"Maybe Vesta can help you," Alex said. "But you need to go to her. She's in the Esmeira palace."

"No one can go to the Esmeira palace unless summoned by the Overseer," Ruok said with a deep sigh, then looked at Alex. "Where are you from? You don't look like you're from anywhere I know of."

"We're from London." Alex replied. 'From the dimension… that only I know how to come from and go back to."

"Could you take me there?" Ruok sat up. "Vezan's killers won't find me there. I can be safe for a while.

"Oh, we…" Scarlette looked worried. "I mean, we don't know anything about you, Ruok."

"Oh, don't worry. I just need a place to quietly hide for a while." Ruok smiled slightly. "And I can tell you about dozens of dimensions where you can go and enjoy yourselves."

"That sounds fun." Alex nodded. "No worries, mate, you can come with me to London."

"Okay." Ruok finished his super burger and a dark-looking brew in one go and stood up. "Let's go… before Vezan's death squads find me."

"Hold on tight." Alex, "Let's go back to London and try them out." Marcus said excitedly.

"Yes, let's do," Scarlette added with the same eagerness.

"And to London we shall go!"

Alex read the magical book to make the supernatural energy take them home.

As the energy of the book enveloped them, Alex, Scarlette, Marcus, and Ruok felt a powerful surge, much like the sensation of being pulled through a vortex.

The world around them blurred and shifted, colours merging and morphing in a whirlwind of light and sound.

Moments later, they found themselves standing on a bustling London street.

Towering skyscrapers, busy pedestrians, and the sounds of honking cars filled the air. Ruok, the cave man from the Thunder Forest World, looked around in amazement, his eyes wide with wonder.

"Is this London?" Ruok asked his voice a mixture of awe and disbelief.

"Yes, welcome to London!" Alex grinned, his excitement mirrored by his friends. "This is where we're from."

Ruok's keen senses were immediately bombarded with the sights, sounds, and scents of the bustling city. The scent of coffee wafted from nearby cafes, mingling with the aroma of street food. Neon signs advertised shops and entertainment venues, and the energy of the city was palpable.

"Wow, this place is incredible!" Ruok exclaimed "So many different scents and sounds."

"Yeah, London is quite the place." Marcus chuckled. "We've got everything from historical landmarks to modern technology."

"But let's not forget why we're here." Scarlette reminded them, glancing at Ruok. "We need to find a safe place for him to hide."

Ruok's expression grew more serious as he nodded. "Right, I appreciate your help. Vezan's hunters could be anywhere, and I don't want to put you in danger."

"We'll do our best to keep you safe." Alex assured him. "But first, let's find a suitable place for you to stay."

The group made their way down the busy streets, passing by iconic landmarks like Big Ben and the London Eye. Along the way, they discussed various options for Ruok's hideout.

"I've heard that there are hidden spaces within old buildings in London," Marcus suggested. "Some of them could be perfect for staying out of sight."

"That sounds like a good idea." Scarlette agreed. "We just need to find one that's abandoned or rarely visited."

As they wandered through the city, they stumbled upon an old, somewhat dilapidated building tucked away in a quieter corner. It had a certain air of mystery about it, and it seemed to have been overlooked by the majority of passers-by.

"This might be it." Alex said, studying the building. "It doesn't seem like it gets much foot traffic, and it's away from the main areas."

The group cautiously entered the building, exploring its interior. They discovered a series of interconnected rooms and hallways, each with a unique atmosphere. Dust motes floated in the air as sunlight streamed in through cracked windows, casting a warm glow over the forgotten space.

"I think we've found our hideout." Ruok said, his eyes gleaming with gratitude.

Over the next few days, the friends helped Ruok settle into his new hideout. They brought supplies, including food, water, and necessities, ensuring he would be comfortable during his stay. They set up makeshift sleeping quarters and fortified the entrances to keep unwanted visitors out.

As Ruok made himself at home, he shared stories of his own world, the Thunder Forest World, and its unique inhabitants and landscapes. Alex, Scarlette, and Marcus were captivated by his tales of adventure and danger, finding themselves drawn into the lore of his dimension.

"We've never met anyone from another dimension before," Marcus admitted. "It's amazing to hear about the different worlds out there."

"I'm glad I could share a piece of my world with you." Ruok said with a smile. "And I'm grateful for your hospitality."

Days turned into weeks, and the friends developed a routine. They would explore different parts of London during the day, showing Ruok the city's vibrant culture and history. In the evenings, they would return to the hidden building to share stories, laugh, and enjoy each other's company.

CHAPTER SIX

DIMENSIONS UNITED

"We made it! I was kinda worried we'd end up in the wrong place."

Alex grinned, feeling a surge of pride. He glanced down at the D-Blasters they had just purchased in the other dimension.

The D-Blasters were remarkable devices, their sleek bodies reflecting a purple shiny, silvery colour. The sun's rays danced off the polished surface, casting an iridescent glow. Strapped to holsters on their backs, the D-Blasters were both practical and visually striking.

The trio had acquired these weapons during their adventures, and now they were a tangible reminder of the challenges they had overcome. The blasters' designs were reminiscent of super soakers but with an otherworldly and futuristic twist.

As they stood in their world once more, Alex couldn't help but run his fingers over the surface of his D-Blaster.

The silvery material felt cool to the touch, and the intricate engravings seemed to tell a story of their own.

With a touch of his finger, Alex activated a holographic display on the blaster's side. A series of buttons and indicators lit up, each labelled with a different symbol. These symbols represented the various blaster streams that the D-Blasters could unleash, each specifically designed to counter different inter- dimensional threats.

"We might be back home," Scarlette mused, her eyes flickering with curiosity, "but it doesn't mean the adventure has to end, right?"

Marcus nodded in agreement, his fingers itching to explore the blaster's buttons. "Definitely. We've got these amazing tools now. Who knows what otherworldly challenges we might face?"

As they exchanged excited glances, they realised that even within the confines of their ordinary reality, the possibilities were endless. With their D-Blasters at the ready, Alex, Marcus, and Scarlette knew that their adventures were far from over

They were still strapped to their belts; a tangible reminder of the adventures they had just embarked upon.

"Yep! We're back, guys. And with some cool souvenirs."

As they stood in the midst of their world, a sense of accomplishment settled over them. They had faced challenges, discovered new dimensions, and acquired powerful tools along the way.

It was a feeling of camaraderie and achievement that was hard to put into words.

"So," Marcus began with a mischievous grin, "who else is dying to share the epic-ness of our adventures with everyone at school?"

Scarlette chuckled. "You mean, let everyone know we've been dimension-hopping and fighting monsters in alternate realities?"

"Exactly!" Marcus nodded enthusiastically. "I mean; how often do you get to do something this awesome?"

"Actually it gets better," he confessed and he pulled out the large silver ghost "Power" coin. His grin returning and explained.

The expressions on Marcus and Scarlette's faces shifted from curiosity to surprise, then to sheer excitement.

"You mean... you've been holding out on us?" Marcus exclaimed, playfully nudging Alex's shoulder.

Scarlette joined in the teasing, her eyes dancing.

Alex laughed, feeling a weight lift off his shoulders.

"Okay, okay, you're right. We're a team and I just couldn't resist sharing the awesomeness with you both."

The trio exchanged stories, laughter, and excited chatter.

They relived their adventures, their encounters with strange creatures, and the breath-taking landscapes of the alternate dimensions.

The challenges and triumphs they had faced together created a bond that seemed unbreakable.

As the sun began to set, casting a warm golden hue across the horizon, their conversation began to shift to a more sombre note.

"Well," Scarlette said with a wistful smile, "I guess it's time to head home."

"Yeah," Marcus agreed, "back to our own reality. But hey, we've got to meet up again soon and find that sceptre, right?"

Alex nodded, feeling a sense of determination. "Definitely. Our adventure isn't over yet. We'll regroup, plan, and get ready to face whatever challenges come our way."

With a final round of goodbyes, the friends parted ways, each heading toward their respective homes.

The sense of anticipation lingered in the air, a promise of future adventures and the unbreakable bond that connected them.

As Alex walked down his street, he couldn't help but feel a surge of gratitude for the extraordinary friends he had by his side.

The ordinary world seemed a bit less ordinary now, knowing that beyond its surface lay countless dimensions, each holding its own wonders and dangers.

With a determined smile, Alex stepped into his house, ready to embrace the familiar routines while holding onto the memories of the dimensions he had explored. The adventure had only just begun, and he couldn't wait to see where it would lead him next.

The next day dawned with a mix of anticipation and curiosity for Alex. With the sun filtering through his bedroom window, he couldn't help but smile at the thought of the newfound powers at his disposal.

He carefully secured the large silver Ghost coin (or "Power Coin" as Dippy liked to call it) with its generic ghost emblem glinting in the morning light, to his necklace and rubbed it with his thumb a few times.

It began to glow and Alex could feel it's power. The potential of the coin fascinated him—it wasn't just about battling monsters;

it was about exploring the limits of what he could do.

As he headed to school, he decided to test the waters by using his temporary ghostly abilities for personal gain. He rubbed it with his thumb as previously instructed, to let its power commence...

The school day progressed as usual until he found himself sitting in Mr. Wills' history class, his mind drifting away from the lecture.

With a subtle grin, he tapped into the power of the coin.

Within moments, he felt himself becoming ethereal, a faint shimmer engulfing his form.

With a light-hearted chuckle, he slipped through the classroom wall, leaving behind a baffled teacher and classmates.

Outside, he soared through the air, a euphoric sensation of flight coursing through his veins.

The world looked different from up high, and he couldn't help but revel in the freedom as he maneuverer among the clouds.

But time was of the essence; the coin's power was temporary.

Alex returned to his human form, re-entering the classroom with an amused smile that masked his secret escapade.

Later in the day, as he strolled through his neighbourhood, he noticed his elderly neighbour struggling to water her plants.

Drawing on his newfound abilities, Alex phased through the garden fence, much to the surprise of the old woman.

He playfully made the watering can levitate and watered the plants, earning a delighted smile and gratitude from his neighbour.

His adventures weren't just limited to benevolent gestures,

However, after school, he decided to use his powers to get back at Lucas and his gang in a way that would leave them annoyed.

During a casual basketball game at the local park, with Lucas towering over his opponents, in full swing, a self-assured grin plastered on his face. The crowd watched, a mix of fear and admiration in their eyes, as Lucas dribbled the ball with a cocky swagger.

As the game reached a crucial point, with Lucas about to score yet another point, Alex's plan sprang into action. With the Ghost coin safely tucked in his pocket, he focused his thoughts on the ball. In a blink of an eye, the ball's trajectory twisted, and it sailed off course, much to everyone's confusion.

Laughter erupted from the onlookers as the ball spun through the air, missing the hoop by a comical margin. Even Lucas stared at the ball in disbelief, his confident expression replaced with a mixture of shock and frustration. Alex couldn't help but smirk, the taste of victory sweet on his tongue.

As the laughter grew louder, Lucas's face flushed red with anger. His aura of invincibility had been shattered, and he couldn't quite comprehend what had just happened. Alex relished the moment, a rare triumph over the tormentor who had made his life miserable for so long.

Yet, amidst the satisfaction, Alex couldn't ignore the twinge of guilt that tugged at his conscience. Deep down, he knew that revenge wasn't the best path to take, that it wouldn't truly satisfy the ache he felt for acceptance and popularity. He had momentarily stooped to Lucas's level, and the victory felt hollow in the grand scheme of things.

Over the following days, as the incident became the talk of the school, Alex grappled with conflicting emotions. On one hand, he had successfully put a dent in Lucas's ego, and the bullying had momentarily subsided.

In moments of quiet introspection, Alex admitted to himself that he didn't want to be popular through intimidation and humiliation. He wanted to be admired for who he was, for his own strengths and talents. It was a revelation that changed his perspective and motivated him to find a more genuine way to gain recognition.

As time went on, Alex continued to explore his powers, not just as a means of revenge. One afternoon, as the sun cast a warm glow over the neighbourhood, Alex strolled through his peaceful surroundings. His thoughts turned to his other elderly neighbour, Mrs Jensen; a gentle woman wearing glasses perched on her nose, and a perpetual twinkle in her kind blue eyes, whose garden always seemed to be in need of tending. The sight of her struggling to water her plants pulled at his heartstrings.

With a smile, Alex reached into his pocket and grasped the Ghost coin. Focusing on his intentions, he gently phased through the garden fence and materialised beside Mrs. Jensen. Her surprised gasp turned into a delighted smile as she watched the watering can float in mid-air, watering her plants with precision.

Mrs. Jensen's eyes sparkled with gratitude, and Alex revelled in the simple joy of making someone's day a little brighter. It wasn't about the recognition or praise it was about using his powers to bring happiness to those around him.

Days turned into a series of magical experiments, each one more creative and heart-warming than the last. He'd turn mundane situations into extraordinary moments, like making a forgotten umbrella float back to its owner during a sudden rainstorm or creating colourful illusions to entertain children at the local park. These acts weren't driven by the need for popularity or revenge; they were fuelled by a genuine desire to add a touch of wonder to the world.

However, Alex's magical exploits weren't limited to benevolent gestures. His rivalry with Lucas persisted, and while he had shifted his focus away from revenge, he still couldn't resist the urge to give Lucas a taste of his own medicine. After school one day, he decided to use his powers to annoy Lucas and his gang in a way that would leave them bewildered.

As Alex continued to use his powers for personal enjoyment and positive purposes, he became more adept at controlling them. He learned that his abilities were a gift, a unique way to connect with the world and make a positive impact. The once burning desire for popularity slowly transformed into a deeper yearning for meaningful connections and genuine experiences.

With every enchanting act, Alex found himself growing more attuned to the world's hidden magic. He revelled in the extraordinary within the ordinary, and he realised that his journey wasn't just about battling monsters or getting even with bullies. It was about exploring the very essence of life itself, adding a touch of enchantment to the mundane, and discovering the beauty that existed all around him.

added a sprinkle of magic to ordinary moments, and, in doing so, started to gain a reputation as someone kind and resourceful.

Alex didn't stop there, when he arrived home, he discovered that his stepdad was about to reprimand him for a minor mishap.

Seizing the opportunity, he activated his ghostly abilities, causing small objects to shift and dance around the room, creating a playful chaos that amplified his stepdad's confusion and anger. Alex laughed to himself.

Days turned into a series of entertaining experiments, each one more creative than the last. He turned mundane situations into magical moments, from swapping Breezy's ice cream cone with a slice of pizza and then switching them back, to making a forgotten umbrella float back to its owner during a sudden rainstorm.

While these exploits brought a sense of fun and mischief, Alex was always careful not to overstep boundaries.

He didn't want to become reckless with his powers and risk revealing his secret to the wrong people.

With every use of the coin, he honed his control and understanding of its capabilities.

As he continued to navigate his world, Alex found that his days were filled with a newfound wonder.

He revelled in the extraordinary within the ordinary, using his powers not just to fight monsters, but to add a touch of enchantment to his everyday life. And with the silver Ghost coin around his neck, he was ready for whatever adventure and misadventure lay ahead.

With each new adventure, he found himself more connected to the world around him, more attuned to the magic that existed beneath the surface of the mundane. His journey had transformed from battling monsters to exploring the very essence of life itself. And as he moved forward, he carried with him the spirit of adventure, curiosity, and the knowledge that even in the ordinary, there was a touch of enchantment waiting to be discovered.

The D-phone began to buzz.

Alex's heart skipped a beat as he retrieved the D-Phone from his pocket and stared at the glowing screen. The device emitted a soft, otherworldly hum as its surface flickered with a holographic image.

It was Vesta, He signalled the others to back away and answered the call.

"Alex Knight?" Vesta's lovely image filled the screen.

"How have you been these last few days?

I have heard strange reports about a boy fitting your description being seen in a few dimensions you should not be in."

"I... I wanted to know more about the dimensions and all these new powers I have."

"Fair enough." Vesta nodded. 'But I hear you were not alone in these endeavours."

"I... I had a few friends with me along., you know the ones you met in Esmeira, in case I would need any help."

"You will be solely responsible if any mishap were to befall them."

"I understand, Vesta." Alex said with a sheepish grin. "I will take full responsibility."

"That's good." Vesta sighed. "But now, the reason why I am contacting you now.

Word has come to me of the one who made the breach that has upset the balance.

An evil dictator by the name of Vezan..."

"Oh Yes, Vezan." Alex yawned.

"What?" Vesta looked concerned. "How do you know of him?"

"Huh?" Alex regained his composure. "No, I mean... I... it sounds like something I heard a long time ago."

"Never mind." Vesta replied. "This evil dictator is rumoured to have opened the Forbidden Dimension and allowed its horrors to spread across all the dimensions everywhere, including yours but he still doesn't have full control of the Forbidden dimension as the sceptre had been accidentally lost in the portals a millennia ago during the magical attempt to hide it from others who may want to obtain it for its power but that's what he's looking for.

Be ready with your weapons and ability.

I will summon you if I need you here."

"I will be ready, Vesta." Alex nodded and hung up.

As Alex hung up the D-Phone, he turned to his friends, Marcus and Scarlette, who had emerged from the shadows of the alley.

"So, everything Ruok said was true," Marcus said, his voice a mixture of awe and excitement.

Alex nodded, his mind racing with the implications of what Vesta had just told him. The threat of an evil dictator named Vezan who had opened the Forbidden Dimension was even more concerning than he had imagined. It wasn't just about battling monsters and exploring alternate realities anymore; it was about safeguarding the very fabric of existence.

"We need to be prepared," Alex said, his voice determined. "If this Vezan has unleashed horrors across all dimensions, we can't afford to underestimate the danger."

Scarlette stepped forward, her eyes filled with a steely resolve. "We've faced challenges before, and we've come out stronger every time. We'll figure out a way to stop Vezan and close that Forbidden Dimension for good."

Marcus clenched his fists, his competitive spirit flaring up. "I'm not letting some evil dictator mess with our world and the other dimensions. We've got these D-Blasters, and we've got each other. We'll take him down."

The trio exchanged a resolute look, their bond stronger than ever.

This was a battle they couldn't shy away from. Their adventures had prepared them for this moment, and they were ready to step up to the challenge.

As they walked out of the alley and into the bustling streets, they discussed their strategy. They needed to gather more information about Vezan, his motives, and the extent of the threat he posed. They also needed to find out if there were any allies they could enlist in their fight against him.

Over the next few Hours, they delved deep into research, both in their world and through the D-Phone's resources, connecting with individuals who had encountered the effects of the Forbidden Dimension's breach. They pieced together a clearer picture of Vezan's tyranny, the horrors he had unleashed, and the devastation he had wrought in various dimensions.

During one of their research sessions, Alex discovered a hidden message encrypted within the D-Phone's data. The message revealed a secret meeting point within an alternate dimension, where individuals from various realities were planning to come together to strategise and form a united front against Vezan.

With the location in mind, Alex, Marcus, and Scarlette gathered their gear and prepared to embark on another inter-dimensional journey. They recited the magic words Vesta had taught them, and the world around them shifted once more. This time, they found themselves in a vast, ethereal landscape, a meeting ground that transcended the boundaries of time and space.

The place was filled with beings from different dimensions, each with their own unique abilities and stories.

Alex's heart swelled with a mix of curiosity and admiration as he observed the gathering. Despite their differences, they were all united by a common purpose: to defeat Vezan and restore balance to the multiverse.

As they mingled with the other individuals, Alex, Marcus, and Scarlette shared their own experiences and learned from the wisdom of those who had faced similar challenges. They discovered new techniques, forged alliances, and gained insights that would prove invaluable in the battle ahead.

One being, a wise and ancient guardian named Lumina, approached them. Her eyes sparkled with a profound understanding of the cosmic forces at play.

"The power to overcome lies within your unity," she said, her voice carrying a weight of authority. "Your friendship, your shared experiences they are your greatest weapons."

With renewed determination, the trio returned to their world, ready to put their knowledge and alliances into action. They trained tirelessly, honing their skills with the D-Blasters and fine-tuning their teamwork. They also spread the word to other like-minded individuals across dimensions, rallying them to the cause.

CHAPTER SEVEN

BOUND BY UNITY: HEROES ARISE

Alex and his friends had decided to spend the day relaxing in a quiet park, enjoying the camaraderie that came with being close friends.

The gentle rustling of leaves and the distant hum of the city created a soothing backdrop to their laughter and conversations.

Lounging on a patch of soft grass, Alex, Scarlette, and Marcus were caught up in their banter when Dippy, the group's tech-savvy member, approached them with an air of urgency.

His fingers tapped anxiously on the sleek tablet he held in his hands.

"Hey, guys," Dippy began, his tone serious. "I hate to interrupt the fun, but I've got some urgent news. Remember those Possessor Gargoyle Viruses we've heard about?"

Alex's eyebrows furrowed as he nodded.

"Yeah, the ones from the Dark Dimension.

What about them?"

Dippy's expression turned grim as he swiped his tablet, displaying an eerie image of sinister creatures.

"Well, it looks like a few of those escaped into our world.

They've taken up residence in a local mall not too far from here. The problem is, they're possessing ordinary items and even food, turning them into dangerous entities that are attacking people."

The atmosphere shifted from carefree to charge with anticipation.

Really? the spark of adventure ignited in their eyes.

Scarlette's voice was laced with determination. "We can't just sit back and let innocent people suffer.

We have to stop those viruses." With a determined nod, Marcus cracked a grin.

"You're right, Scarlette. It's time to show these Possessor Gargoyles what we're made of."

Alex's gaze remained fixed on the tablet screen, his mind racing.

"Dippy, do you have any more details about the situation at the mall?"

Dippy nodded, tapping on his tablet. "I've got a live feed from the mall's security cameras. Things are escalating quickly. People are panicking, and the possessed items are causing chaos everywhere. Oh and Ruok is there by the way but he is eating chicken and chips not at all appearing to be bothered by the commotion"

The sense of urgency united them in a common purpose.

They rose to their feet, a palpable energy coursing through the air.

Their once-relaxed demeanor was now charged with a mix of excitement and apprehension. As they reached the entrance of the mall, they were met with a chaotic scene.

Panicked voices, the clatter of running feet, and the occasional shriek filled the air.

"So Ruok is in that mall?" Scarlette asked Alex amused as they ran out of the alley and toward the local shopping mall.

"Yes, he is." Alex nodded with a grin. "He wanted to mingle and understand more about our culture, so I told him the best place to do that would be in a crowded place, like this mall."

"And what about the way he looks?" Marcus scratched his head.

"People will think he's just another weirdo in a furry mask." Alex laughed and pointed ahead. "And look, there is Ruok..."

Ruok turned around at the sound of his name, smiling wide with his mouth half-full whilst eating his chicken and chips. "You were right, Alex Knight. This mall is such a wonderful place; I feel like a Londoner already. I've never tasted chicken like this before and these chips are quite extraordinary"

"That's swell." Alex smiled back. "Now the dictator will never be able to find you."

"Oh great." Marcus tugged at Alex's sleeve. "You spoke too soon; I think they found his minions already."

"What are those things?" Scarlette's eyes went wide at the sight of several Gargoyle like creatures began appearing out of thin air.

"Oh no." Ruok cried out with fear in his eyes. "The Possessor Virus!"

"Crikey!" Alex and Scarlette yelled together.

Ruok continued. "The dictator must have sent the virus here. The Virus strains possess their victims and make them do evil things." "We have to stop them." Alex swung the D-Blaster from its strap into his hands. "This D-Blaster can send them back to where they came from."

"Are you sure?" Scarlette asked as she and Marcus also aimed their D-Blasters at the ugly Gargoyle.

"Alex is right." Ruok shook his head. "You can shoot the virus Gargoyle back to the forbidden dimension with your D-Blasters."

Scarlette clenched her fists, her resolve unwavering. "We've got to put a stop to this before more people get hurt."

Alex's eyes glinted with determination as he activated his D-Blaster, its futuristic design gleaming. "Remember, our shots can only affect the Possessor Gargoyles. Our priority is to protect the innocent."

Marcus raised his D-Blaster, his grip firm. "Got it. Let's clear this place up."

With an unspoken agreement, they ventured deeper into the mall, the sounds of chaos growing louder, the once serene atmosphere of the mall had transformed into a scene of chaos and terror. Possessed items lurched and lunged, their malicious intent evident in every movement.

Alex, Scarlette, and Marcus stood at the heart of the frenzy, their D-Blasters at the ready.

With each shot they fired, a Possessor Gargoyle vanished, but the onslaught seemed unending.

As they moved through the mall, more objects came to life, each one a threat.

Alex, Marcus, and Scarlette stood at the forefront of the battle, flanked by beings from various dimensions. The air was charged with anticipation as they faced Possessor Gargoyles and his horde of horrors.

With a battle cry, they unleashed the full power of their D-Blasters, combining their abilities in a dazzling display of light and energy.

The battle raged on, each pulse of energy pushing back the darkness, each united effort chipping away at Possessor Gargoyles forces.

But the Possessor Gargoyles going down without a fight. He emerged from the chaos, a formidable figure wreathed in malevolent energy. A fierce battle ensued, the clash of powers shaking the very foundation of reality.

Where is Ruok?" Alex thought. He seemed to briefly disappear for the majority of the battle.

In the midst of the battle, Lumina's words echoed in Alex's mind. Their unity was their greatest weapon.

Drawing strength from their friendship and shared experiences, Alex, Marcus, and Scarlette poured every ounce of their determination into the fight.

The battle was intense, filled with twists and turns, moments of despair and glimmers of hope. It pushed them to their limits, testing their resolve and challenging their abilities. Possessed mannequins writhed with unnatural life, arms flailing and legs jerking. Clothing racks whirled like dervishes, flinging hangers and garments with surprising force.

Scarlette narrowly dodged a possessed potted plant that lunged at her like a carnivorous predator, its tendrils reaching out with a menacing snap.

A group of possessed shopping carts careened down an escalator, their metal frames clanging against the steps as they gained speed. Alex, Marcus, and Scarlette were forced to scatter, leaping over railings and ducking behind pillars to avoid the crashing onslaught.

Amid the chaos, an unholy symphony of sound emerged. The possessed pianos hammered discordant melodies, while chairs danced and tables flipped, creating barriers that made their progress treacherous.

Dippy's tablet buzzed with real-time security feeds, offering a glimpse of the pandemonium that had erupted. Possessed concession stands spewed popcorn like machine gun fire, while frizzy fountains sprayed sticky liquid in erratic bursts, making the floor treacherous.

Customers screamed and fled, their panicked footsteps mingling with the cacophony of destruction.

Alex, Scarlette, and Marcus had their hands full as they fended off the relentless onslaught. But for every creature they dispatched, two more seemed to take its place.

Scarlette's voice quivered with a mixture of frustration and desperation. "We need to find the source of these Possessor Gargoyles and put a stop to this madness!"

Amidst the chaos, a possessed merry-go-round whirled to life, its painted horses galloping wildly. It charged toward them, carousel music warping into an eerie, distorted melody.

Alex leapt onto a passing shopping cart, riding it like a makeshift chariot, while Marcus and Scarlette used their D-Blasters to create makeshift barriers, forcing the merry-go-round to a grinding halt.

As the battle raged on, fatigue began to wear on their resolve.

Alex's brow glistened with sweat as he dodged a possessed bicycle rack that came hurtling his way, its wheels spinning with malevolent speed.

The constant barrage of attacks began to take its toll, leaving them breathless and battered.

In a desperate bid to regroup, they converged near a towering sculpture in the centre of the mall.

even this haven proved temporary as possessed drones buzzed overhead, their propellers spinning like saw blades.

The sculpture itself seemed to come alive, its metallic limbs reaching out with surprising agility.

Dippy's voice crackled over their communicators, cutting through the cacophony.

"Hey, everyone, listen up!" Dippy's voice carried a sense of urgency. "I've been analysing the D-Blasters' data while you were fighting, and it turns out these weapons aren't just effective against the Possessor Gargoyles."

"What do you mean?" Scarlette asked, her voice tense.

Dippy's voice continued, the excitement evident. "The D-Blasters shoot a concentrated stream of inter-dimensional energy that works on all sorts of creatures from other dimensions. It's not just limited to the Possessor Gargoyles. The stream has a water-like property that can conduct electrical energy through any inter-dimensional entity, disrupting their molecular structure."

A spark of realisation ignited in Alex's eyes as he absorbed the information. "So, you're saying the D-Blasters can neutralise any inter-dimensional threat, not just the Possessor Viruses?"

"Exactly!" Dippy affirmed. "It's like an electrical shock that messes with their composition. Remember that the inter-dimensional plane operates differently from our world, so this type of energy can destabilise them."

The news opened up new possibilities in the midst of their battle.

Scarlette's voice held a hint of hope. "So, if we focus our D-Blaster shots on the other creatures, we might be able to neutralise them as well?"

"Exactly!" Dippy reiterated. "It's worth a shot. Try focusing your shots on the core or the centre of the creatures. The energy should disrupt their molecular bonds and send them back to their own dimensions."

Amidst the chaos, the trio adjusted their tactics. Their D-Blasters crackled with energy as they fired targeted shots at the possessed objects that surrounded them. With each hit, sparks flew, and the objects convulsed before dissipating in a burst of inter-dimensional energy.

A possessed shopping cart charged toward them, its wheels spinning wildly. Scarlette adjusted her aim and fired a focused shot at the heart of the cart. The energy raced along its metal frame, causing it to shudder and finally disintegrate into a burst of light.

Alex's eyes gleamed with determination as he aimed his D-Blaster at a possessed umbrella stand that had sprouted sinister tentacle-like appendages. He fired a stream of water-like energy, and the tentacles spasmed before evaporating into thin air.

As the battle raged on, the possessed items were no longer invincible adversaries; their molecular structures were destabilised by the energy coursing through them.

Dippy's voice crackled again, "Guys, I've isolated the epicentre of these Possessor Gargoyles. It's in the mall's atrium. But it won't be easy. The source seems to be well-guarded."

With renewed determination, they pushed forward, navigating through a storm of chaos. The possessed escalators clanged and groaned, trying to trip them up, while swirling gusts of wind created by possessed ceiling fans buffeted their every move.

Finally, they reached the atrium, where a massive Possessor Gargoyle loomed over a swirling vortex of dark energy. Possessed banners twisted and twirled around it, adding to the spectacle. The Gargoyle's eyes glowed with malevolence, its wings stretching wide as it summoned even more possessed objects to its aid.

The battle reached its climax as Alex, Scarlette, and Marcus unleashed a barrage of shots at the colossal Gargoyle. Explosions of light and energy illuminated the atrium, sending shockwaves that rippled through the air. The possessed items that had seemed invincible moments ago crumbled and disintegrated, and the vortex's pull weakened.

But the Gargoyle fought back with newfound fury, launching tendrils of dark energy that lashed out like whips.

The trio struggled to evade the attacks, their movements growing sluggish.

Scarlette was knocked off her feet, and Marcus was ensnared by a dark tendril, the air squeezed from his lungs.

Desperation etched across his face, Alex focused his energy, his silver ghost coin glowing brightly. With a surge of power, he fired a concentrated blast that struck the Gargoyle's core, causing it to roar in agony. The vortex faltered, and with a final defiant howl, the Possessor Gargoyle shattered into a burst of dark energy.

The atrium fell silent, the chaos subsiding as the vortex collapsed upon itself. Panting and bruised, Alex, Scarlette, and Marcus stood victorious but weary, their D-Blasters now quiet. Dippy's voice crackled once more, relief evident in his tone.

"You did it! The mall's returning to normal. You guys are amazing."

As the dust settled and the possessed items reverted to their inert forms, a collective sigh of relief rippled through the mall. Shoppers emerged from hiding places, their expressions a mix of gratitude and awe.

Scarlette wiped sweat from her brow, her voice a mix of exhaustion and triumph.

"We did it. But man, that was close."

Alex nodded, a wry smile playing on his lips.

Their victory was met with applause from the crowd that had gathered.

As the mall's chaos gave way to an air of gratitude and relief, the three friends exchanged a knowing glance. They had faced danger head-on, confronted their limitations, and emerged stronger for it. The adventure had tested their bonds and their courage, but they had prevailed,

A loud cheer went up from all the people in the mall as the mall began to return to a state of normalcy, the adventure etched itself into their memories.

Their triumph served as a reminder of their resilience, a testament to the unbreakable bond they shared. The memory of that chaotic battle would forever be a testament to their unity and determination, a shining example of how, even in the face of danger, they could prevail against all odds.

"Everyone's going to know about this." Marcus said as he put his D-Blaster aside.

"Alex, you're a hero." Scarlette ran up to him as he floated down again.

But Alex didn't respond. He looked a little disoriented, as if he didn't know where he was. His eyes were very dark and hollow. Then he shook his head and grinned, back as he was before.

"What was that?" Marcus asked him. "What happened to you?"

"Don't know." Alex shrugged. "Felt a little weird for a bit…"

"It's Alex's new powers from the Ghost Coins." Ruok said to them. "If your use too much, it can affect you negatively. Have a strawberry brew, it'll make you feel better."

"For that we need to get to that bar back in the inter-dimensional portal station." Scarlette said.

"So, do let's." Marcus grinned. "I can eat half a dozen of those delicious super burgers."

"And a dozens of those Donuts." Alex nodded happily as he recites the magical rhymes and, in a flash, the three of them disappeared.

The days that followed the mall incident buzzed with a newfound energy. The news of Alex and his friends' heroic efforts had spread like wildfire, earning them not only local fame but also respect among their peers.

Dippy's edited highlight reel had gone viral, showcasing the heart-pounding battle against the Possessor Gargoyles and capturing the raw determination that had fuelled their victory.

Social media platforms were abuzz with discussions about the extraordinary events at the mall. Comments, likes, and shares flooded in, and hashtags like #TeamHeroes and #MallBattle trended for days. Alex, Scarlette, Marcus, and even Ruok found themselves recognised on the streets and approached by awestruck fans, eager for selfies and autographs.

Breezy, who had always harboured a not-so-secret crush on Alex, seemed to be among their most enthusiastic admirers.

Her infatuation had transformed into something of a full-blown obsession since news of their heroic feat broke out. She attended the same school as Alex, and her presence seemed to follow him everywhere, much to his amusement and occasional discomfort.

On sunny afternoon, as Alex and Scarlette sat on a bench outside the school, Breezy appeared seemingly out of nowhere, her eyes wide with admiration. She twirled a strand of her hair, a nervous giggle escaping her lips. When she wasn't around Lucas she tended to show her true feelings for him.

"Hey, Alex! You were so amazing at the mall. Can I get a picture with you?"

Alex exchanged a knowing glance with Scarlette before offering a friendly smile.

"Sure thing, Breezy. Just remember, we're just regular people who happened to be in the right place at the right time."

As Breezy excitedly posed for a selfie with Alex, Scarlette leaned closer to him, her lips curving into a playful grin.

"You know; I think you might have a secret admirer."

Alex chuckled, shaking his head. "Yeah, it's hard to miss. I appreciate the support, but it's a little overwhelming."

Their laughter was interrupted by a commotion nearby. A group of students had gathered around a bulletin board plastered with flyers advertising a "Heroic Celebration Carnival," an event organised to honour Alex and his friends for their heroic deeds. Alex scratched his head, bemused by the attention. "Looks like things are getting even bigger."

As the day of the carnival approached, anticipation built among the students and the local community. The event promised a day of entertainment, games, and activities, all centred around celebrating the courage and unity that had driven Alex and his friends to face down danger.

The atmosphere was charged with excitement as the carnival grounds took shape, with colourful banners, food stalls, and a stage for live performances.

On the day of the carnival, the sun shone brightly, casting a warm glow over the festivities. The air buzzed with laughter, music, and the joyous chatter of attendees. Families, students, and even tourists had gathered to partake in the celebration, united by a common sense of admiration for the young heroes.

Alex and his friends mingled with the crowd, their faces a blend of excitement and humility.

Scarlette nudged Alex with a playful smile as they walked past a food stall.

"Remember, we're here to have fun too, not just be on display."

Alex grinned, a mischievous glint in his eyes.

"Don't worry, Scarlette. I've got my eye on those cotton candy machines."

As they indulged in carnival games and treats, Breezy managed to find them once again. Her eyes sparkled as she clutched a bouquet of flowers.

"Alex, you were amazing at the mall, and I just wanted to say that you're my hero."

Alex accepted the flowers confusedly.

"Erm thank you, Breezy" and Scarlette held back her giggle. As the day progressed, the carnival's main stage came to life with performances by local bands and dancers. The highlight of the event was a heartfelt speech by the mayor, acknowledging Alex and his friends for their bravery and selflessness. The crowd erupted into applause, their appreciation resonating throughout the carnival grounds.

Amid the festivities, Ruok approached Alex, his eyes twinkling with amusement. "Looks like you're quite the celebrity now."

Alex shrugged, a mix of gratitude and humility in his expression. "It's a little overwhelming, but I'm glad we could make a difference."

Ruok's gaze turned serious. "Remember, with great power comes great responsibility. It's not just about the recognition, but how you use your abilities to help others."

As the sun began to set, casting a warm orange glow over the carnival, Alex and his friends took the stage once more. The crowd hushed, their attention focused on the group that had captured their hearts. Alex stepped forward, his voice steady and sincere.

"We didn't set out to be heroes. We were just friends, hanging out and enjoying life. But when the moment called for it, we faced danger together. We fought not because we had superpowers, but because we cared about the people around us."

The crowd listened intently, hanging onto every word. Alex's gaze shifted to his friends, a sense of camaraderie and gratitude welling within him.

"Our strength comes from each other; from the bond we share.

So, to all of you, thank you for being here and reminding us that unity and courage can make a difference."

The applause that followed was thunderous, echoing the sentiment that had brought everyone together.

Amidst the laughter and music, Alex caught sight of a familiar face in the crowd. It was Mr. Johnson, the old librarian who had always encouraged his love for books and learning. With a grateful smile, Alex excused himself from the dancing and made his way over to the older man.

"Mr. Johnson, I didn't expect to see you here," Alex said, extending his hand.

Mr. Johnson shook his hand warmly. "Well, Alex, I couldn't miss the chance to celebrate your courage and achievements. You've come a long way from the quiet student who used to spend hours in the library."

Alex chuckled. "Yeah, I guess I have."

"Remember, Alex, heroes come in all forms. It's not just about possessing extraordinary powers, but about having the heart to use them for the greater good," Mr. Johnson said with a knowing smile.

Alex nodded, his gaze drifting back to his friends who were still dancing and enjoying the festivities. "You're right. It's not just about the powers; it's about what we do with them."

As the night deepened, the carnival's atmosphere shifted from bustling excitement to a more serene ambiance.

The lights twinkled like stars overhead, and a bonfire crackled in a corner, casting a warm glow. Groups of friends gathered around the fire, sharing stories and laughter.

Alex, Scarlette, and Marcus found themselves by the bonfire, their expressions a mix of contentment and camaraderie.

Ruok, having found a comfortable spot, joined them, his eyes reflecting the dance of the flames.

"You know," Marcus mused, "this whole hero thing is pretty surreal.

One day, we're just hanging out, and the next, we're saving the world."

Scarlette chuckled. "Well, it's not like we asked for it, but I'm glad we were able to step up when it mattered."

Ruok nodded in agreement. "The path of heroes is often unexpected, but it's how we navigate that path that defines us."

As they shared their thoughts, Breezy approached, her enthusiasm still undiminished. "What does this girl want?" Alex thought. She carried a plate of s'mores and offered one to Alex with a shy smile.

"I thought you might be hungry," she said, her cheeks pink.

"Thanks, Breezy," Alex replied, accepting the treat but also still confused. Breezy was an entirely different person when she wasn't with Lucas. Breezy shrugged, a bashful grin on her face. "Well, heroes deserve all the support they can get."

The group laughed, their spirits buoyed by the warmth of the fire and the camaraderie of the night. As the hours ticked by, they continued to share stories, dreams, and even their fears. As the carnival came to a close, the group gathered one last time near the bonfire.

The night sky was dotted with stars, a reminder that even in the darkness, there was always a glimmer of hope.

"We've been through a lot," Scarlette said, her voice soft but resolute. "But we've also come out stronger and we have each other."

Alex nodded, his gaze sweeping over his friends. "We may not know what challenges lie ahead, but as long as we stick together, there's nothing we can't face."

Ruok raised his cup in a toast. "To unity, courage, and the unbreakable bonds that define us."

The others raised their cups as well, clinking them together in a shared moment of solidarity.

As they gazed into the fire, they knew that their journey was far from over, but they were ready to face whatever came their way.

The carnival's embers slowly faded, leaving behind a sense of fulfilment and purpose and as Alex, Scarlette, Marcus, Ruok, and even Breezy bid the night goodbye, they carried with them the lessons of unity, courage, and the unwavering belief that even ordinary individuals could be heroes.

CHAPTER EIGHT

"BONDS OF ADVENTURE: A TALE OF FRIENDSHIP AND CHOICES"

The next day, Alex, Marcus, and Scarlette decided to chill themselves at a quaint outdoor café, nestled amidst the lively bustle of the city.

The aroma of freshly brewed coffee and delectable pastries wafted through the air, mingling with the laughter of locals and the distant hum of traffic. The trio had managed to find a cosy corner, away from the prying eyes of strangers, where they could share their secrets and dreams.

Alex took a sip of his steaming cup of coffee, relishing its rich and invigorating taste.

"You know," he began, leaning back in his chair, "I sometimes wish this was our reality all the time – no villains, no ancient prophecies, just friends enjoying life."

Marcus grinned, his eyes twinkling with mischief.

"Oh, but where's the fun in that? Adventures make life interesting."

Scarlette chuckled, her gaze shifting between her two friends.

"And our lives are anything but boring, that's for sure."

Alex nodded, his thoughts drifting to their recent escapades.

"Remember that time at school when Lucas tried to make a fool out of me?"

Marcus smirked. "Oh, how could we forget? You stood your ground though."

"Thanks to you guys," Alex said, his expression softening. "You've always had my back."

Scarlette reached over and playfully nudged Alex's shoulder. "That's what friends do, Alex. We're a team."

As they chatted, the conversation turned to Alex's stepdad.

"How's everything at home, Alex?" Marcus asked, genuine concern in his voice.

Alex sighed, his expression clouding over slightly.

"Well, you know, it's been a bit rocky. My stepdad and I haven't really been seeing eye to eye lately."

Scarlette leaned forward, her expression sympathetic.

"It's tough adjusting to a new family dynamic."

"Yeah," Alex replied, his gaze dropping to his cup. "But at least I have you guys to talk to."

The atmosphere shifted as they delved into lighter topics.

"And what about Breezy?" Marcus quipped, a knowing smile on his face.

Alex chuckled, a playful glint in his eye. "Oh, she's still following me around, dropping hints and blowing kisses. I don't know if I should be flattered or concerned."

Scarlette laughed, shaking her head. "Well, at least you've got an admirer."

Their conversation meandered through stories of Ruok's efforts to blend into modern London society while avoiding Vezan's clutches.

"It's a bit like a spy movie," Marcus mused. "Ruok hiding in plain sight."

Alex nodded, a grin tugging at his lips.

"And the way he struggles with modern technology is both hilarious and endearing."

As they sipped their drinks and savoured the delicacies, the friends also speculated on the whereabouts of the ancient sceptre.

"Do you think it's really hidden somewhere in London?" Scarlette pondered aloud.

"Who knows?" Alex mused. "But one thing's for sure – we'll keep searching until we find it.

We owe it to Esmeria."

Their camaraderie was palpable, their connection stronger than ever. As the sun dipped below the horizon, casting a warm golden glow over the city, Alex felt a deep sense of gratitude for the friends who had stood by him through thick and thin.

"We'll face whatever comes our way together," Marcus declared, raising his cup in a toast.

Scarlette and Alex joined in, clinking their cups together. "To friendship and adventure," Scarlette added with a smile.

"To Esmeria and beyond," Alex said, a spark of determination in his eyes.

In that moment, the trio's laughter and shared stories echoed through the lively streets, a testament to the bonds they had forged and the challenges they were ready to confront.

The next school day, Lucas, the school's resident bully, began to change his tone.

He had been one of Alex's most relentless tormentors, but now he was suddenly interested in Alex's powers. He approached Alex one morning, his tone surprisingly friendly, though the scepticism in his eyes was unmistakable.

"Alex Knight, the super hero." Lucas laughed at Alex as he stood before the school building.

"Yes, he is." Marcus replied.

"Alex is chosen for greatness." Scarlette added. "And we're helping him."

"So, what's your superhero name?" Lucas snorted. "What powers do you have?"

"I can do anything I want." Alex glared at the bully.

"Can you beat up Brian?" Lucas patted his large friend's thick arm.

"I don't have those kind of superpowers." Alex explained. "I can fight beings from another dimension…"

"Other dimension?" Breezy looked puzzled.

"Like ghosts." Marcus grinned, clearly enjoying the big girl's confusion.

"No exactly ghosts." Alex said with a straight face. "But beings from another dimension… I can go to these dimensions and get powers and rewards…"

"Sounds boring." Lucas yawned. "Look, you want to be cool and not get picked on anymore, come to the pool party at the cool kid's club and show us what your powers can do, then you can hang with the coolest gang in London."

"You can do it, Alex." Breezy blew him a kiss as the bullies walked away. "I know you can."

"Don't do it, Alex." Scarlette hissed as soon as the bullies were out of earshot. "You'll only make a fool of yourself in front of those snobs."

"Scarlette's right, Alex." Marcus pitched in. "It's not worth it. Even if they let you join their cool club, it'll only be because they want to show off that a famous kid is a member of their snooty club."

"Yeah, Alex." Scarlette added. "It's not Alex Knight whom they want, it's what you can do. Totally not worth it."

"I know you two mean well..." Alex said with a shake of his head. "But you don't know how long I wanted to hang with the coolest kids in school, and this is my best chance. I'll have them eating out of my hand."

"Trust you to be a fool, Alex." Scarlette shook her head in dismay.

"Yeah, as usual." Marcus nodded in agreement. "Would be much better if you'd spend the time between dimension hopping on doing your homework assignment..."

"You know what? You two are just jealous of my powers!" Alex said defiantly. "Fine then, the two of you can do what you like but I'm not missing out. I'll head to this party myself then!"

"But Alex..." Scarlette cried out.

"Leave him be, Scarlette." Marcus held her back. "He'll find out the hard way as usual."

Alex found himself standing at a crossroads, torn between his aspirations of being recognised by the popular crowd and his deep-seated loyalty to his best friends, Marcus and Scarlette.

He gazed down at the invitation to the pool party, Lucas' handwriting staring back at him.

A sense of apprehension crept over him, a nagging feeling that perhaps this was not the path he should be taking.

The allure of the party was undeniable. It was a chance to shed his former identity and emerge as the hero he envisioned himself to be.

The thought of demonstrating his unique powers to the popular crowd filled him with a thrilling anticipation.

But just as quickly, doubts seeped into his mind. What if I stumbled?

What if he faltered in front of everyone?

The cautionary words of Scarlette echoed in his thoughts, reminding him of the potential embarrassment that awaited him.

He cast a glance at his D-Phone, the mysterious device that linked him to his alternate dimension abilities. Its screen remained dark, mirroring his uncertainty. Yet, a more profound thought surfaced, the value of the friendship he shared with Marcus and Scarlette.

While the allure of being accepted by the cool kids tugged at him, he couldn't dismiss the bond he had cultivated with his steadfast companions.

Through the many twists and turns of their adventures, Marcus and Scarlette had been his pillars of support. They had stood by him, believed in him, and lifted him up when self-doubt threatened to pull him down.

With a decisive exhale, Alex stowed the D-Phone away, his heart now leaning toward a different choice.

He acknowledged his reservations, fears, and pride, yet he also recognised the treasure of true friendship he possessed.

"Guys," he began as he met up with Marcus and Scarlette later that day, "I want you to know how much I appreciate our friendship.

You've been there for me through thick and thin, and I'm grateful for that."

Marcus raised an eyebrow, sharing a puzzled glance with Scarlette.

"Is this the real Alex or a shape-shifting imposter?"

Alex chuckled, a bashful smile forming. "No, it's me. I've been doing some thinking.

You both were right; I shouldn't be so focused on impressing those cool kids.

Our friendship means too much to me."

Scarlette's eyes softened, a relieved smile spreading across her face.

"We're relieved you see it that way, Alex. No matter what, we're here for you."

"Yeah," Marcus added, "We might not always agree, but we've got your back."

Alex nodded, his heart swelling with warmth. "Thanks, guys.

You have no idea how much your support means to me."

As the sun began its descent, casting a golden glow over the city, Alex extended an invitation. "I know the party scene isn't your thing, but I'd love for you to come, not as my sidekicks, but as my friends."

Scarlette offered a disappointed look "Thanks Alex but we'll pass. You just go and have your adventure with the popular kids." She said sarcastically.

Their refusal was a testament to their principles, but he couldn't help feeling a twinge of disappointment. He would be venturing into this experience alone, stepping into a realm unfamiliar to him, while his friends stayed true to their own convictions.

And so, as the stars began to twinkle in the evening sky, Alex set forth toward the pool party.

A blend of excitement and trepidation stirred within him.

Flying into the pool party would be a grand entrance, he thought.

That would get him instant points with the cool crowd. He shot off in the direction of the pool party, soaring over the streets of London.

Then suddenly he felt very tired and found himself falling back down. He steadied himself and realised that there was a limit to his powers.

"Better save my supernatural energy for the party." He told himself. "Especially since I've used too much of this power coin."

Alex regretted having not listen to with his two best friends. But then they just didn't understand how much he wanted to be cool and popular, and this was his only chance. After a few more minutes of walking, Alex arrived at the site of the pool party.

Lucas was already there and waved in him past the gate.

Alex nodded in appreciation as Lucas grabbed him by the arm and dragged him to the centre of the party.

"Look who's here." Lucas held up Alex's arm.

"London's very own super hero, former nerd and video game junkie, Alex Knight."

"Is it true you have super powers?" A dizzy blonde in a red swimsuit gushed close to him.

"Show us your powers." Another girl shouted from the back.

"Yeah. Show us your powers." A tall young man whom Alex recognised as the host of the party and the coolest kid in London shouted.

The chant picked up and soon everyone there in the party shouted his name and urged him to show them his super powers.

Alex took a deep breath and closed his eyes. He felt like he was a rock star on the stage about to belt out his latest hit single. He leaned back and snapped his fingers; the supernatural energy should make him teleport from one end of the pool to the other. But nothing happened. He focused his energy to make himself fly, but realised his Power Ghost Coin was currently recharging and he had already used up too much of its powers…

The D-Phone was his last chance and he flipped it out. But it wasn't lit. It never needed charging, so why was it not working.

The gathered pool party crowd began to get impatient. A few boos began creeping into the cheers. Alex looked around and realised he was making a grand ass out of himself. He realised that his best friends were right and he was wrong as the boos began to get louder.

"He's a phoney." Someone yelled.

"Get him out of here." Another shouted.

"You'll pay for this, Knight." Lucas grabbed him by the collar and pushed him out of the front gate. "You made a fool of me..."

"Of you?" Alex shouted in anger. "I made a bigger fool out of myself..."

"Just get the dickens out of here while you can, worm food." Lucas spat and slammed the gate.

"Arghh, I'm so mad right now..." Alex kicked at the gate, hurting his own foot more than the iron bars. "Now I have to get back to Marcus and Scarlette and tell them I'm sorry... I am such a blooming idiot."

"No, I am not." A voice burst inside his head. "I am not an idiot."

"What? Who is this?" Alex looked around in shock. "Show yourself."

"I am you and you are me." The gruff voice laughed.

"What? What?" Alex felt his heart beating faster. "How can... this is a trick."

"Look in that puddle of water in the drain." The voice inside his head told him.

Warily Alex peered down at the stagnant water in the drain and had a great shock. He didn't see his own reflection. Well, it was him, but quite a bit different. He looked rather hideous, as if he was being transformed into an Orc or an Ogre, or both. Something like the playable character he'd design for himself in a video game.

"Who is that?" Alex gasped. "That is not me."

"That is me." The mean voice in his head laughed. "I am you and you are me. I am your alter-ego. I am Lexa."

"What?" Alex nearly fell off his feet. "That can't be... I can't a have an evil alter ego."

"The more you use the Large Ghost Coins and your power irresponsibly, the more you feed me." Lexa laughed inside his head. "And soon I will take over, and Alex Knight will be no more."

"No! No!" Alex yelled and began running. "I've got to find Marcus and Scarlette... they're my only hope."

Breathless and heart pounding, Alex sprinted through the streets, his thoughts a chaotic whirlwind.

The weight of his actions hung heavy on his shoulders, and his mind replayed the moment of humiliation at the party over and over again. I needed to find Marcus and Scarlette, to seek their understanding and forgiveness, to mend the bonds that his reckless pursuit of fame had strained.

Alex's words tumbled out in a rush, his guilt and regret pouring forth as he found himself teetering on the edge between his normal self and the malevolent alter ego he had come to know as Lexa.

The lines between these two personalities were blurring, leaving him bewildered and anxious about his own identity.

Every surge of power within him brought a surge of fear, and he struggled to grasp control over the raging storm that brewed within.

Alex returned home to the stern presence of his stepdad. This time, however, his stepdad's anger wasn't directed solely at his late arrival. Instead, it centred on the destruction and chaos that had followed him due to his unstable powers.

His stepdad, oblivious to Alex's fame and abilities, saw only the aftermath of a disaster.

"Alex, I've had enough of your reckless behaviour!" his stepdad bellowed, his face a mask of frustration and disappointment.

Alex, his mind a jumble of confusion and guilt, struggled to find words to defend himself.

He knew the havoc his powers had wrought, but he was powerless to stop it.

As his stepdad's scolding words washed over him, a feeling of powerlessness and frustration surged within him, a feeling that was becoming all too familiar.

And then it happened. In the blink of an eye, the transformation took place once more. The contours of Alex's face twisted, his eyes darkening as they glinted with malice.

His stepdad's voice faltered as he witnessed the startling change before him. The once-familiar features were replaced by a malevolent and terrifying visage.

Lexa stood before his stepdad, a sinister grin playing on his lips.

"Are you challenging me?" Lexa's voice was deep with an unsettling mix of amusement and menace.

His stepdad's heart raced as a chilling shiver ran down his spine. He couldn't believe his eyes – this was a nightmare straight out of a horror story. Panic gripped him, and he turned and fled, slamming the door to his room behind him.

Inside the room, Lexa's laughter echoed through the walls, a bone-chilling sound that reverberated in the air. But as the seconds passed, the laughter faded, and Lexa's sinister presence dissolved.

In its place stood Alex, his hands trembling and his heart pounding. The transformation back to his true self had occurred just as unexpectedly as the previous change.

Shaken to his core, Alex sank to the floor, his head in his hands. He was trapped in a nightmarish cycle, and he had no idea how to escape it. It wasn't just about the chaos he was inadvertently causing – it was the fear of losing himself entirely.

As Alex struggled with his inner turmoil, Dippy appeared before him, a flicker of concern in his eyes. He gently placed a paw on his shoulder, and a sense of comfort flowed through him.

"Alex, I know this is hard, but you can't let this consume you.

Your friends need you now more than ever." Alex looked up, his eyes reflecting his doubt and self-blame.

"Dippy, you don't understand. I can't control this. I'm a danger to everyone."

Dippy's gaze held unwavering determination.

"True friends see beyond the darkness, Alex. They believe in you even when you can't believe in yourself. Don't forget that."

(Meanwhile, Scarlette and Marcus had been doing some research of their own in search of the sceptre since Alex followed his will to party with Lucas at the pool.)

They had stumbled upon stories and legends about a powerful artefact known as the Sceptre of Equilibrium. Rumoured to grant its wielder immense power, the sceptre had the potential to reshape reality itself.

Intrigued by the idea of harnessing its power for good, Marcus and Scarlette decided to embark on a quest to find the sceptre, their determination fuelled by the desire to prove their worth and independence since Alex had betrayed their friendship.

(As they delved into ancient texts and sought out hidden clues, their bond strengthened, and their resolve deepened.)

The next day, Alex's friends huddled in the dimly lit school library, poring over ancient texts and dusty tomes in search of information about the Magical Sceptre.

The tension between them and Alex still lingered in the air, like a fog that refused to lift.

Alex stood on the periphery, watching them with a mixture of longing and regret.

As they pieced together their findings, the theory emerged the Magical Sceptre had likely been hidden all along, within the depths of the Natural History Museum in London.

The revelation sent a wave of excitement through the group, drawing them into animated discussions and theories.

The prospect of finally ending this dangerous chapter filled them with renewed determination.

Summoning all his courage, Alex approached his friends, his heart pounding. He tried to act like everything was normal, that the rift between them had never occurred.

"Hey, guys," he began tentatively, his voice barely above a whisper.

"Mind if I join you?"

The group fell silent, their gazes locked on Alex. Marcus, normally quick with a response, averted his eyes, and Scarlette's lips tightened into a thin line.

The tension was palpable. As Marcus opened his mouth to speak, Scarlette shot him a pointed look, causing him to close it abruptly. The unspoken tension between Alex and his friends seemed to hang in the air like a heavy cloud.

Alex sighed inwardly, the weight of his mistakes pressing down on him. "Look, I know I messed up, but you have to listen to me now. You're in grave danger if you go after the sceptre on your own."

The hesitation was evident in Marcus's eyes, but Scarlette's voice cut through the uncertainty. "Alex, we don't need your warnings or your help. We've got this covered."

The rejection stung, but Alex understood their perspective. He nodded solemnly, his shoulders slumping as he turned away.

The pain of losing their trust and friendship cut deeper than he could have imagined. As he walked away, a soft voice reached him. it was Marcus, his voice hesitant but resolute.

"Alex, just go. We can handle this ourselves."

Despite the ache in his heart, Alex couldn't help but admire their determination, even if it came at the cost of their friendship. He gave a single nod and left the library, a sense of emptiness gnawing at him.

Unbeknownst to them all, a student sitting at a nearby table had overheard their conversation.

This student happened to be a member of Lucas' gang, and the information he had overheard was too valuable to keep to himself.

He discreetly informed the high-level members of "The Hood" about the plan to retrieve the sceptre from the Natural History Museum.

The gears of Lucas' gang began to turn as they hatched a daring scheme to inform the high level members of The Hood to infiltrate the museum and get the powerful sceptre. The high level members' plan was to pose as well-dressed guests as they planned to stage a robbery under the guise of sophistication.

Little did they know that their actions were about to set in motion a chain of events that would reveal a traitor among their ranks.

As Marcus and Scarlette continued their research, they overheard snippets of conversation from fellow students. One voice stood out, a student discussing The Hoods' plan with excitement and intrigue.

The revelation hit them like a bolt of lightning. The Hood was planning to steal the sceptre from the museum, and they had to stop them before it was too late.

The duo sprang into action. They knew they needed someone on the inside to thwart The Hoods' plans, and that someone was Ruok, the mysterious being, that Marcus and his friend had been harbouring.

Before the night of the heist, Marcus and Scarlette put their plan into motion. In their quest to uncover the sceptre, Marcus and Scarlette devised a daring scheme to infiltrate The Hood. They knew that if they were to retrieve the sceptre, return it to Esmeira and save the world, they would need an insider who could navigate the treacherous underworld and that insider was none other than Ruok, they had no other plan than to him join the crew.

They had been harbouring Ruok in their shed, away from prying eyes and curious of Vezan.

They knew that Ruok's unique abilities and his connection to the other dimension could prove invaluable in their mission but first, they had to transformed him into someone unrecognisable, someone who could blend in seamlessly with the members of The Hood.

Ruok stood in front of a cracked mirror in Marcus' shed, attempting to adopt the persona of a British cockney gangster. He wore a mismatched suit that looked a bit too tight on him, attempting to emulate the style of the criminal underworld.

Scarlette and Marcus watched with a mix of amusement and encouragement.

"Ohh! guv'nor! Look at me, all dressed up and ready to dive into the underworld," Ruok said in his best cockney accent, giving himself an exaggerated wink in the mirror.

Scarlette couldn't help but laugh. "You look like you raided a thrift store in a hurry."

Ruok grinned, catching a glimpse of his reflection. "Well, blending is all about embracing the character, innit"

Marcus chimed in, "Remember, Ruok, you need to make sure your backstory is convincing. Tell them you've got a connection to The Hood something that would make them believe you're one of them."

Ruok nodded, his expression shifting from amusement to focus. "Right, I've got it. I used to run with a crew back in me old haunt, and I've got a mate who owes me a favour or two. That should do the trick."

With his backstory in place, Ruok was ready for his introduction to the high-level members of "The Hood."

Ruok, disguised as a British cockney gangster, dialect, they made their way to an inconspicuous meeting spot, where Marcus had arranged the encounter. They waited in the shadows as Ruok walked into the headquarters of "The Hood." the group of imposing figures, his cockney accent in full swing.

"'Hello, mates!" Ruok greeted them, "I'm 'ere to join the crew, I am," Ruok proclaimed, doing his best to adopt the accent. He paused, catching himself slipping into his natural Shakespearean his voice dripping with exaggerated slang. "Got wind of this place from a bloke I know. Heard you lot are the real deal, innit?"

The gang members exchanged glances, clearly taken aback by Ruok's over-the-top performance. One of them, a burly man with a scarred face, stepped forward. "Who's this then? Another wanna-be trying to impress us?"

Ruok quickly improvised, his cockney accent wobbling slightly. "Nah, nah, mate. Been around the block a few times, I 'ave. You might know me old pal, Snickers? We used to knock around together, we did."

The gang members regarded Ruok with scepticism, clearly unsure whether to believe his story. Ruok felt the tension in the air and caught himself slipping out of character.

"Well, ain't this a fine mess," he muttered under his breath, his accent momentarily fading into his natural Shakespearean dialect.

The gang members exchanged puzzled glances, raising their eyebrows in confusion. "What did you just say?" one of them asked.

Ruok cleared his throat, his face flushing. "I mean, 'course, mate. Just talking' a bit, I was. You know how it is."

The gang members shrugged, seemingly satisfied. "Alright, mate. You're in. I know snickers but you better prove your loyalty. We've got a job tonight, and you're coming along."

With a nod of agreement, "Alright, mates," Ruok's voice crackled through the walkie talkie. "I've got my eyes on the prize, and I must say, it's an extravagant beauty"

"Ruok, are you alright?" Scarlette's voice sounded concerned. "You're slipping out of character."

Ruok quickly caught himself, his accent returning to its exaggerated cockney form. "Just a bit of a mix-up, luv. I'm right as rain, I am."

Ruok was now officially part of the gang's plan. He communicated with Marcus and Scarlette via walkie talkie, detailing the gang's every move as they prepared for the heist at the museum.

The night was alive with tension as the gang of criminals known as "The Hood" prepared to carry out their audacious heist on the city's most secure museum. The Natural History Museum. Ruok, disguised in his makeshift cockney gangster persona, stood at the forefront, his heart pounding with a mixture of excitement and apprehension. The dim glow of streetlights illuminated their faces as they assembled outside the museum's imposing walls.

The leader of the gang, spoke in hushed tones, outlining the plan one last time. "Remember, this is our one shot at getting that sceptre. The museum's security is top-notch, but we've got a few tricks up our sleeves. Stick to the plan, and we'll be walking out with a fortune tonight."

The group shared nods of agreement, their eyes gleaming with a mixture of greed and determination. As they entered a sleek black van and prowled through the labyrinth like roads. The van was adorned with tinted windows, an emblem of "The Hood" etched onto its side – a symbol of their illicit prowess.

Inside the van, the atmosphere was charged with a mixture of excitement and tension. The members of the gang, each dressed in dark attire, exchanged knowing glances and whispers. The Enforcer, the charismatic but ruthless leader, sat at the forefront, his fingers tapping against the armrest in rhythm with the impending heist.

Beside him sat Ruok, who had seamlessly adopted his carefully crafted cockney gangster persona. The transformation was both amusing and unsettling Ruok's typically elegant and regal demeanour now cloaked in an over-the-top facade.

Ruok shifted uncomfortably in his ill-fitting suit, his movements awkward and exaggerated as he tried to embody the characteristics of a British gangster. He occasionally muttered cockney slang under his breath, practicing his newfound identity.

"Oi, guv'nor," Ruok mumbled, his voice betraying an undercurrent of Shakespearean eloquence. He quickly caught himself and cleared his throat, reverting to his affected cockney accent.

The leader cast an amused glance at Ruok. "You sure about this, new blood? You look like you're wearing a suit two sizes too small."

Ruok's lips twitched, a hint of his natural self-threatening to break through. "Right, right! Tight fit for a proper gangster, innit?"

The leader chuckled, satisfied with Ruok's commissions. "Just remember, we're going in there for one thing – that sceptre. You grab it, and you'll be one of us for real."

The van came to a stop near the museum's perimeter, shrouded in darkness and anticipation. The gang members disembarked, their footsteps purposeful and resolute. The night's cool breeze seemed to carry a whisper of danger, a reminder of the stakes that awaited them.

The leader led the way, his eyes locked on the museum's entrance. Ruok followed, his movements a careful balance between his newly adopted persona and his true self. As they approached the entrance, The Enforcer cast a final glance at Ruok. "Remember, mate, act the part and this'll be a breeze."

Ruok nodded, a nervous smile tugging at the corners of his lips. The entrance loomed before them, a portal into uncertainty. With a deep breath, they crossed the threshold, stepping into the heart of the mission that would determine the course of their destinies.

Security cameras blinked overhead, their mechanical eyes shrivelling every movement. The gang moved with practiced precision, evading the cameras' gaze and slipping deeper into the museum's interior. The tension in the air grew palpable, the weight of their objective bearing down on them.

Ruok's heart raced as they ventured further into the maze of corridors. His borrowed accent wavered at times, threatening to expose his true identity. He exchanged furtive glances with the gang members, offering an apologetic grin whenever his cover slipped.

Their journey brought them to a room bathed in the soft glow of emergency lights. The atmosphere was laden with the scent of history, the air thick with anticipation. The display case holding the Sceptre stood before them, its lasers casting an ethereal dance.

Ruok took a deep breath, his fingers trembling slightly as he tapped at the handheld device he had hidden within his pocket. The lasers flickered and faltered, their once-deadly barriers now rendered powerless.

As the display case opened, revealing the ancient sceptre After a heart-pounding pursuit, Ruok reached the display holding the ancient sceptre.

With the ancient sceptre secured, Ruok felt a surge of both exhilaration and trepidation. The display room had been a labyrinth of lasers and security measures, but his supernatural abilities had allowed him to navigate through with uncanny grace. The sceptre itself held a mysterious allure – a tangible connection to a world he had long been separated from.

As Ruok made his way through the dimly lit corridors, he could hear the distant sounds of alarms echoing through the halls. He moved with purpose, his steps quick and deliberate, knowing that the gang members who had accompanied him were facing their own challenges.

In another part of the museum, chaos erupted as the gang members encountered the security measures. The alarms blared, casting a red hue over the scene as they struggled to evade the lasers and surveillance systems. The Enforcer,, his normally composed demeanour fraying at the edges, barked orders and directed his team in a desperate attempt to bypass the obstacles.

However, despite their best efforts, some members of the gang were caught by the security systems. Their movements triggered blaring alarms and flashing lights, drawing the attention of both security personnel and their criminal counterparts. The tension escalated as guards closed in, creating a frenzy of evasive manoeuvres and adrenaline-fuelled escapes.

Amidst the chaos, Ruok's path converged with Marcus and Scarlette's in the car park. Their faces lit up with a mixture of relief and excitement as they saw Ruok approaching, the sceptre cradled carefully in his hands.

"Ruok, you did it!" Marcus exclaimed, his voice a mixture of astonishment and pride.

Scarlette's eyes sparkled with admiration. "You really pulled it off!"

Ruok nodded, his lips curving into a smile that held a trace of the genuine camaraderie he had formed with them. However, that smile quickly faded, replaced by a chilling intensity as his true intentions revealed themselves.

The air around Ruok seemed to darken, a palpable shift in his demeanour that sent a shiver down their spines. The transformation was swift, as if a veil had been lifted to expose the sinister underbelly that lay beneath his façade.

Before Marcus and Scarlette could react, Ruok's gaze hardened and his fingers twitched with malevolent energy. A shock blast erupted from his palm, the surge of power catching them off guard. The force of the blast sent them sprawling to the ground, pain and confusion coursing through their bodies.

As they struggled to regain their bearings, they looked up to see Ruok standing over them, his once-amiable expression replaced by a chilling smile. His voice dripped with malice as he spoke, his words a jarring juxtaposition to the friend they thought they knew.

"Such trusting fools," Ruok mused, his tone dripping with scorn. "You really believed I was on your side?"

Marcus pushed himself to his feet, his gaze locked on Ruok with a mixture of disbelief and anger. "Ruok, what are you doing?"

Scarlette, her voice a mixture of fear and betrayal, managed to rise as well. "Why? We trusted you!"

Ruok's laughter echoed through the car park, a haunting sound that sent a chill down their spines. "Trust is a weakness, my dear friends. And weakness will be your downfall."

With a flick of his wrist, Ruok summoned a surge of dark energy, his malevolent powers crackling around him like a tempest. Marcus and Scarlette's hearts raced as they realised the depth of their predicament they were facing a threat far more dangerous than they could have ever imagined. Just as they were about to muster a response Ruok struck them down. As he attempted to fire again, a familiar figure burst onto the scene.

Alex, his expression a mix of determination and concern, as he held a D-Blaster in his hand. He positioned himself between Ruok and his fallen friends with his D-Blaster pointed at Ruok and his voice unwavering as he spoke.

"This ends now Ruok," He shot his D-blaster and the blast knocked Ruok down unconscious.

Marcus stood up and walked up to Alex.

"You saved us, Alex." Marcus said with a frown. "I decided never to speak to you.

again, but I owe you my life now."

"Nonsense, Marcus." Alex hugged his best friend. "We're friends for life."

"Scarlette, I knew i messed up. I let my desire for fame and popularity cloud my judgement.

I thought I could impress everyone with my powers, but they failed me, and I ended up making a fool of myself."

Marcus's expression softened, his concern shifting to empathy.

"Alex, we tried to warn you. Fame and popularity aren't worth sacrificing who you are and the relationships that matter."

Tears welled up in Alex's eyes, his voice choked with emotion. "You were right; I should have listened.

Alex nodded, his throat tight with emotion. "I know I messed up. I just... I wanted to be accepted, to finally be someone people admired."

Scarlette sighed, her gaze softening. "Alex, being admired for the wrong reasons isn't worth it.

True friends don't care about your powers or fame; they care about who you are."

"We're angry because you let us down, Scarlette's expression softened.

Also, we are sorry and apologise for not listening to your warning concerning the search of the sceptre on our own.

"What's happened to your face?"

Marcus noticed the harsh lines and bumps on Alex's features.

"You look kind of evil."

"I know." Alex said. "Using my powers too much can make me evil.

"Alex?" Scarlette yelled, "Is that you? You look so weird."

"Yes, it's me. Using too much of my powers makes me look like this.""

I need our combined powers to get us to the dimension hub and have some of that strawberry brew; it's the only thing than can get me back to normal or the sceptre"

"I'm sorry, Scarlette." Alex looked down at the ground. "I need the two of you... together our powers combined will help me control what's happening to me."

"How do you know that?" Scarlette inquired.

"Dippy told me." Alex held up the D-Phone. "Now let's get the sceptre from Ruok"

As they were discussing, Ruok's eyes opened and grin widened, his eyes ablaze with a dark energy that seemed to defy the very laws of nature. In a wisp of smoke and shadows, he vanished, leaving behind a sense of foreboding and uncertainty.

As the echoes of his laughter faded into the night, Marcus, Scarlette, and Alex were left to grapple with the harsh reality that their friend had deceived them.

Alex knew it was time to reveal what he had deduced about Ruok's true intentions during the planning stages of the heist. He recounted the conversations, the subtle hints, and the actions that had raised suspicion in his mind.

"Remember when you were planning the heist?" Alex began, his voice steady. "Ruok always seemed a bit too eager, too focused on the sceptre's power. It was like he had a personal stake in it, beyond just the fame or the treasure."

Scarlette nodded thoughtfully. "I remember feeling that something was off about him, but I couldn't put my finger on it."

"That's not all," Alex continued, his gaze unwavering. "I got Dippy to spy on the whole ordeal and Dippy informed me that Ruok was the one who suggested the display room, where the sceptre was kept. He knew about the security measures, as if he had insider information and during the heist, Dippy mentioned seeing him navigating through those lasers with uncanny ease."

Marcus's brow furrowed as realisation dawned. "So, you're saying he knew about the security because he had been there before."

"Yes," Alex affirmed. "It wasn't just that. Dippy noticed that Ruok seemed more interested in obtaining the sceptre for himself. He was willing to put us at risk, even if it meant taking down his own teammates."

Scarlette's eyes widened. "You think he used the entire heist to get his hands on the sceptre for his own purposes?"

Alex nodded solemnly. "I do and his actions tonight confirmed it. He previously only had limited powers that allowed him to release the virus from the dark dimension to distract us, keep us busy and out of his way whilst he looked for the sceptre! Ruok must've supernaturally sensed that the sceptre had ended up in London through the portals during the magical battle to obtain it but he just didn't know where. Whilst Vezan is a dictator, he doesn't desire the sceptre for himself because he's aware of the danger it's power can cause to our worlds. Ruok has put this false story out there about Vezan's motives for looking for him. Those in Esmeria have got it all wrong, it's not Vezan but it's Ruok who wanted the sceptre for a darker purpose, something tied to that forbidden dimension and I think that Vezan is out to stop him!"

Marcus clenched his fists, his determination renewed. "Then we need to stop him, before he unleashes more chaos upon the city."

Alex's lips curved into a determined smile. "We will. Together, we have the power to counter him and protect this city.

(*The sceptre, once a symbol of hope, had become a catalyst for a new and dangerous threat one that would test the limits of their courage and determination.*)

In the distance, the wail of police sirens grew louder, a reminder that time was running out. As they slowly rose to their feet, a newfound determination burned in their eyes. The battle against Ruok had only just begun, and they were ready to face the challenges ahead, both in the tangible world and the dark dimension from which Ruok had emerged.

A few minutes later, Alex regained his boyish look and felt no trace of his evil alter ego Lexa within him. He hoped never to experience that horror again.

"Wow! You need to be more careful about how you use the powers." Marcus said.

"Incoming message." Dippy the D-Phone suddenly announced.

"From who?" Alex held up the phone to his face.

"The Overseer Vesta." Dippy replied and the image of the queen filled the screen.

"Alex Knight." Vesta said. "I hope this message reaches you in time. We've had word that it was Ruok who wanted the sceptre for his own purposes. He has plans to unleash all the evil from the Forbidden Dimension. Your city of London will be the first place to be hit. The evil of the Forbidden Dimension is being led there for some reason. You must be ready to defend your city. Remember to use all that you have learned wisely. Fare well. I will meet you soon."

"Blimey!" Marcus stood up. "London is in danger."

"Not if we can help it." Alex said. "Come on, let's get back home."

In a flash the three of them were back in the wet and dark streets of London. Not too many people were out. Alex asked the D-Phone to check local news stations. After a few tries, Dippy found a station. The announcer sounded a bit hysterical.

"It's a virus of some sort." She was screaming. "People are going stark raving mad. It's as if everyone is being possessed by parasites and becoming monsters."

The toxic vampires prowled with an eerie grace, their lizard-like tongues darting out like serpents seeking their next meal. These grotesque creatures moved with a predatory precision, their glowing eyes fixated on unsuspecting individuals who wandered too close. The night air was thick with an aura of malevolence, and a sense of impending dread hung heavily.

As a victim unwittingly ventured near, the toxic vampire would strike with a lightning-fast motion, its long, slimy tongue extending like a coiled spring. Their tongues wrap around the victim, ensnaring them in a slimy, vice-like grip. The prey's struggles were futile as the toxic vampire's grip tightened, its insidious grasp unyielding.

With its prey caught, the vampire's mouth suddenly stretches open, its jaw contorting in an unnatural display of flexibility. A disconcerting screech, piercing and unsettling, emanate from the vampire's gaping maw, echoing through the night like a harbinger of doom. The screech was a haunting sound, an auditory signal of the impending assault on the victim's energy.

Simultaneously, the toxic vampire releases a noxious gas from its enlarged mouth. The gas, thick and sickly green, envelop the victim, suffusing the air with a toxic aura. As the gas settled over the prey, it begins to drain the life force, the very essence of their being. The victim's vitality wane as if being leeched away, and their colours would fade, leaving them a pallid, ghostly figure.

The victim's shock and terror frozen in place as the toxic gas worked its insidious magic. The energy within them waver, faltering like a flickering flame about to be extinguished. As the gas continued its relentless assault, the victim's body tremble, their life force drawn forth until they were on the brink of collapse.

In the final moments of the process, as the victim's strength waned to its limit, they collapse to the ground, their bodies frozen in a state of shock. The toxic vampire withdraws its twisted tongue, the prey's energy now fully drained. The victim's once-vibrant eyes stare blankly ahead, their colour and vitality stolen, leaving behind a husk-like figure.

The toxic vampire, having completed its macabre feast, stand over its victim with a predatory satisfaction. The stolen energy suffuses the vampire's form, its once-pale features gaining a sickly, otherworldly glow. As the toxic vampire absorbed the stolen life force, its body undergo a grotesque transformation, its skin stretching and contorting to accommodate the newfound energy.

The victim, now reduced to a lifeless shell as they become one of the toxic vampires after their transformation was completed.

The cycle continues, as the toxic vampires prowled the night, their lizard-like tongues seeking out more prey, and their disconcerting screeches echoing through the darkness, a chilling testament to the darkness that had been unleashed upon the city.

Ruok has channelled his dark energy through the sceptre. The air crackled with malevolent power as a portal to the forbidden dimension tore open before him. Out of the portal emerged a swirling darkness, a vortex of malevolence that seemed to seep into every crevice of the world around it.

Ruok's eyes gleamed with wicked satisfaction as he released more of the evil possessor viruses from the dark dimension. These vile entities, infused with the dark magic of the sceptre, were designed to take over the minds and bodies of unsuspecting victims, turning them into toxic vampires – creatures driven by insatiable cravings for power, chaos, and blood.

The viruses spread like a plague, seeking out individuals throughout the city. People going about their evening routines suddenly found themselves overcome by an inexplicable darkness that settled into their minds. Their eyes glazed over with an otherworldly glow as the viruses took hold, corrupting their thoughts and desires.

As the first victims succumbed to the virus's influence, they underwent a grotesque transformation. Their once-human features contorted and mutated, their bodies becoming more vampiric in nature. Fangs elongated, skin took on a sickly pale hue, and their nails turned into sharp talons. The once-bustling streets of London soon became a scene of horror, as the newly turned toxic vampires roamed, searching for more victims to join their ranks.

News of the sudden outbreak spread like wildfire, and panic gripped the city. Emergency services were overwhelmed, struggling to contain the rapidly spreading chaos. Citizens barricaded themselves indoors, fearing the malevolent creatures that prowled the streets.

Marcus, Scarlette, and Alex stood in an alleyway overlooking the city, their faces etched with concern and determination. The gravity of the situation was undeniable the danger was no longer limited to the artefact itself, but to the very hearts and minds of the people they cared about.

"We have to do something," Scarlette said, her voice tense with urgency. "We can't let Ruok's plan succeed."

Alex nodded in agreement, his jaw set with resolve. "Vesta's warning was clear. We need to use our powers wisely to counteract the effects of the virus and contain the spread."

Marcus clenched his fists, his gaze hardening as he stared out at the chaos below. "And we have to find Ruok. He's behind all of this."

With a shared sense of purpose, the three friends focused their thoughts and energies. Alex, Scarlette and Marcus hummed their D-Blasters with strength and agility in their ready to face the evil possessor viruses from the dark dimension which turns people into Toxic Vampires.

As the first wave of toxic vampires approached, the trio held their D-Blasters aloft. The devices glowed with an intense light, forming a barrier of protective energy around them. The vampires hissed and recoiled, their twisted features contorting with rage as they encountered the opposing force.

Scarlette's hands trembled, but she steadied her grip on her D-Blaster. Her mind raced, recalling the lessons she had learned about controlling her powers. She focused on projecting a calming aura, hoping to counteract the virulent influence that had overtaken the creatures.

Alex's eyes blazed with determination as he channelled his energy into his D-Blaster. The air crackled with electricity as bolts of energy shot forth, striking the vampires and causing them to convulse in pain. His power surged, pushing back the advancing horde.

Marcus stood at the centre, his stance firm and unwavering. He summoned his strength, sending shockwaves of energy through the ground. The shockwaves disrupted the vampires' balance, making it harder for them to coordinate their attacks.

Together, the three friends fought back the toxic vampires with a combination of focused energy blasts, barriers, and strategic shock waves. The battle was fierce, the air filled with the sizzle of magic and the pained cries of the vampires.

Hours passed, and the trio's stamina began to wane. The toxic vampires showed no signs of relenting, but neither did

Marcus, Scarlette, and Alex. Their determination only grew stronger as they fought to protect their city and its inhabitants.

As the first rays of dawn began to break through the night sky, the vampires' resistance weakened. Scarlette's calming aura seemed to have a gradual effect, chipping away at the darkness within them. Alex's relentless energy bolts had taken a toll on their strength, and Marcus's shockwaves had disrupted their coordination.

With one final surge of power, the three friends launched a united assault. Their D-Blasters glowed brighter than ever, illuminating the alleyway with their radiant energy. The toxic vampires let out anguished cries as they were engulfed by the overpowering light.

"And there must be more in numbers of the virus that we haven't seen before." Scarlette added. "...judging by the hysteria."

"I need to call Mum and tell her to stay indoors." Alex said and dialled the number for home. Someone answered but only grunts and shrieks were all he heard. "Oh No! I think my Mum and stepdad are possessed by the virus."

"That means everyone we know could be possessed." Scarlette gasped. "Oh this is bad, really bad"

CHAPTER NINE

THE VEIL OF SHADOWS

(The air was heavy with a sense of foreboding. Alex's heart raced, his instincts screaming that something was amiss. He had heard whispers and seen the signs that led him to believe the dreaded Toxic vampires were no longer confined)

The clock on the wall ticked ominously, each beat echoing like a distant drum. Alex's stepfather, Paul, sat on the couch, his eyes vacant and distant. The room felt strangely cold, the temperature dropping to an unsettling degree, as Alex's mum, Joanna Knight, entered the room, her brows knitted in concern.

"Paul, darling, are you alright?" she inquired softly, her voice tinged with worry.

There was a strange rustling in the air, almost like a whispering wind. Alex's step dad, Paul, slowly turned his head to face Joanna Knight his wife, but it was not the man she knew that looked back at her. His eyes glowed with an eerie, unnatural light, a malevolent aura emanating from him.

A shiver ran down Joanna Knight, Alex's mum, spine as a sensation of dread gripped her. "Paul, please, talk to me. What's wrong?"

In response, Alex's stepdad, lips twisted into a sinister smile, revealing unnaturally elongated fangs that glinted with a malefic sheen. His once familiar features were contorted by an otherworldly force, his visage distorted into a grotesque mask of horror.

Joanna Knight breath caught in her throat, her voice barely a whisper. "No... This can't be happening."

But it was happening. A cacophony of eerie whispers filled the room, mingling with the ominous ticking of the clock. Alex's stepdad transformation was nearing completion, his body twitching and jerking as if struggling to contain the malevolent force within.

Desperation etched across her face, Joanna Knight staggered back, bumping into a table. Her eyes widened in horror as the lights flickered and the room plunged into darkness for a split second, only to return with an eerie, dim glow.

The transformation was complete. Paul's elongated tongue darted out like a snake, wrapping around Alex's mum wrist in a vice-like grip. His mouth unhinged, his jaw stretching impossibly wide, and

Frozen in shock, Joanna Knight eyes widened as her skin paled and colour drained from her cheeks. She was paralysed, trapped in the vice-like grip of the Toxic vampire's hold. Her mind screamed, her thoughts a whirlwind of terror.

But then, just as abruptly as it began, the grip loosened, and the gas dissipated into the air. Joanna Knight collapsed to the floor, gasping for breath as she regained control of her limbs.

Her heart raced, her mind racing to make sense of the nightmare she had just endured.

With newfound strength, she scrambled to her feet, her instincts driving her to flee the hellish scene before her. Without a backward glance, she rushed out of the room, the chilling whispers echoing in her ears.

As the door slammed shut behind her, she stumbled through the hallways of their home, her breath ragged and heart pounding. She had managed to escape the clutches of her possessed husband, but the image of his monstrous transformation was seared into her memory. She needed to find safety, to make sense of what had just transpired.

As she reached the front door, a gust of cold wind swept through the house, carrying with it an unsettling whisper. She glanced back, half-expecting to see Paul standing there with those malevolent eyes. But the hallway was empty, the only evidence of the recent horror being the lingering sense of dread.

Joanna Knight hesitated, torn between fleeing into the night and staying to confront the nightmare that had unfolded. Her maternal instincts won out, and with a deep breath, she pushed open the front door and stepped out onto the porch.

As the moon hung low in the sky, casting an eerie glow over the landscape. Joanna Knight breath formed misty clouds in the frigid air as she scanned her surroundings. She needed help, guidance, anything that could shed light on the darkness that had infiltrated her home.

A flicker of movement caught her attention. Across the street, a dim light glowed from the window of the old widow's house. Mrs. Hawthorne was known in the town for her deep knowledge of the occult and the supernatural. In her desperation, Joanna Knight knew she had to seek her out, to unravel the mysteries that had torn her family apart.

With determination fuelling her steps, Joanna Knight crossed the street and knocked on Mrs. Hawthorne's door. The seconds that ticked by felt like an eternity, the weight of her fear and uncertainty pressing down on her chest. Finally, the door creaked open, revealing the elderly widow's wise and weathered face.

"Joanna Knight, my child," Mrs. Hawthorne spoke in a voice that seemed to echo with ancient wisdom. "I sensed the disturbance. Come in."

Joanna Knight stepped inside, her eyes scanning the dimly lit room. Peculiar artefacts adorned the shelves, and a faint scent of incense hung in the air. Joanna Knight recounted the horrifying events that had unfolded in her home, from Paul's who is Alex's stepdad, possession to his transformation into something nightmarish.

Mrs. Hawthorne listened intently, her expression grave. "You've encountered the Toxic vampires. They are ancient, malevolent beings that feed on fear and despair. Possessing a host allows them to manifest in our realm."

Joanna Knight hands trembled as she absorbed the gravity of the situation. "Is there a way to free Paul from their grip?"

Mrs. Hawthorne's eyes softened. "There is a ritual, but it's dangerous. We must act quickly before the possession becomes irreversible." The ritual will only maximise his condition.

Joanna Knight nodded, determination etched across her face. She was willing to do whatever it took to save her husband, to banish the darkness that had taken hold of him.

The room was aglow with the soft light of candles, their flickering flames casting dancing shadows on the walls.

Joanna Knight and Mrs. Hawthorne had meticulously arranged symbols and artefacts around the room, each item carefully chosen to aid in the delicate task ahead. The air was thick with the scent of incense, mingling with an undercurrent of tension.

Alex's mum hands trembled slightly as she held an ancient text, its pages filled with cryptic symbols and incantations. Mrs. Hawthorne stood by her side, her eyes fixed on the preparations, her years of knowledge guiding their every move.

"We are about to tread into realms unknown, Joanna Knight," Mrs. Hawthorne spoke softly, her voice carrying a weight of both caution and resolve. "The ritual requires both mental strength and unwavering intent.

Do you understand?" Joanna Knight, her heart pounding in her chest. She was willing to do whatever it took to free Paul from the grasp of the Toxic vampires, even if it meant delving into the supernatural.

As the old woman began to chant the ancient incantations, a soft hum filled the air, growing in intensity with each repetition. Joanna Knight closed her eyes, her mind focused on her love for husband, on the life they had built together. She envisioned his smile, his laughter, the warmth of his embrace. Love was her anchor, and she clung to it with every fibre of her being.

The room seemed to vibrate with energy, the air crackling with an otherworldly power. Shadows danced on the walls, seemingly alive with a spectral dance. Joanna Knight voice wavered for a moment, doubt creeping in, but she pushed it aside, letting her love for her husband, Paul, guided her.

In her mind's eye, she saw Paul as she remembered him, his kind eyes, his gentle touch. But the image began to distort, twisting into the monstrous form he had become.

The memory was painful, but Joanna Knight refused to let fear consume her. She summoned her courage, her voice growing stronger once again.

Outside, the wind picked up, howling like a mournful spirit. The very fabric of reality seemed to tremble, as if the forces they were manipulating were pushing back. But Joanna Knight and Mrs. Hawthorne held steadfast, their wills intertwining in a desperate battle against the malevolent presence.

As the incantation reached its crescendo, the symbols on the floor began to glow with an ethereal light, casting an otherworldly glow on Alex's mum determined face.

She felt a surge of energy coursing through her, a surge of power that seemed to transcend the mundane world.

And then, as quickly as it had begun, the room fell silent. The candles flickered once and extinguished, plunging them into darkness. Joanna Knight heart raced as she opened her eyes, unsure of what had transpired.

"Joanna Knight," Mrs. Hawthorne's voice was calm but filled with concern, "I sense a shift, a weakening of the toxic presence. But we must remain vigilant. The battle is not yet won."

Joanna Knight breath caught in her throat as the darkness seemed to take on a tangible form, a swirling mass of malevolent energy. And then, amidst the shadows, a figure emerged, the form of Paul, his features contorted in a painful struggle.

"Joanna Knight," his voice was a whisper, laced with anguish. "Help me."

Joanna Knight's heart ached at the sight of her husband trapped in this nightmarish state. With renewed determination, she stepped forward, her voice infused with love and conviction. "Paul, remember who you are. Fight against the darkness that holds you!"

The room trembled as the battle raged within James, his eyes flickering between their usual warmth and the eerie, malevolent glow. Joanna Knight words seemed to pierce through the haze, a beacon of hope amidst the despair.

Slowly, painfully, Paul's features began to shift back to their familiar form. His body trembled, his struggle evident in every line of his face. Margaret reached out a trembling hand, her fingers brushing against his.

"Paul, I love you," she said, her voice unwavering. "Come back to me."

And then, as if a dam had burst, the darkness receded, dissipating like a fog lifting with the dawn. Paul's form solidified, his eyes returning to their usual warmth. He staggered forward, collapsing into his wife arms, his breath ragged and weary.

Joanna Knight held him close, tears streaming down her face.

As the battle was intense, The D-Phone said in a high-pitched squeal. "those lizard-like, pale skinned, sharp toothed monsters are Energy Vampires from the Forbidden Dimension." "Look out for yourselves, those long tongues of theirs can paralyse you and suck out your life force."

"If those things are from the Forbidden Dimension, then we can send them back with our D-Blasters!" Alex said excitedly and the gang continued firing away.

CHAPTER TEN

"DIMENSIONAL CONVERGENCE: DEFENDING AGAINST DARKNESS"

Moments later the battle had seemingly ceased with the majority of the Toxic Vampires defeated and retreating. All was quiet for now as the friends were catching their breaths.

"What do we do now?" Marcus looked at Alex.

"We need to find Ruok," Alex responded, his gaze focused on the horizon ahead. "He's tied up in all of this, and we can't afford to let him slip away."

Scarlette nodded in agreement, her fiery hair catching the faint light. If we don't act fast, who knows what could happen?"

"Find Ruok." Alex told the D-Phone.

"Looking." Dippy replied. "Looking' Searching."

"Hurry, Dippy," Alex urged, the urgency palpable in his voice. Every second counted in this dangerous game.

"I found him," Dippy announced, relief evident in its electronic tone.

"Ruok's at a mall close to Trafalgar Square."

"Let's go." As they run to the mall, the group wasted no time, sprinting through the dimly lit streets toward their destination. The street around them was eerily quiet, an unsettling contrast to the chaos that had become their new normal.

"There's the mall." Marcus pointed as they popped up on the street in front of the square. "And it looks normal."

"Yes, the people here aren't in any panic." Scarlette said. "Nor are they doing crazy things."

"You'd think they don't listen to the news." Alex shook his head. "Come on, let's look for Ruok."

Alex let out a sigh, his brow furrowed. "It's like they're oblivious to the larger threat looming over us. Let's not waste any more time; we need to find Ruok before it's too late."

Navigating the mall's corridors, they walked cautiously, scanning the surroundings for any sign of the wild looking man from the Thunder Forest Dimension.

Finally, they spotted him, standing amidst the crowd.

"Hello, Ruok," Alex called out, his voice carrying a mix of curiosity and urgency.

Ruok turned to face them, his eyes revealing a complex mix of emotions. "I see you've found me," he said, his voice a blend of calm and weariness.

The atmosphere grew tense as they confronted the enigmatic figure. However, their focus was soon diverted by an astonishing transformation.

They were surprised with the nature of Ruok as he had become wolf monster.

Ruok's fingers convulsed, his nails growing into dark, curved claws that glinted in the moonlight. The sinews of his muscles bulged and shifted beneath his skin, a visceral reminder of the ancient forces at play. He sank to his knees, a guttural growl escaping his lips as his form contorted in a painful and unnatural dance.

A shadow fell over his body, the moonlight casting eerie patterns across his changing figure. His clothing torn as his limbs elongated, dark fur erupting from his pores like a tide of night.

His features stretched and reshaped, his nose extending into a lupine snout lined with dagger-like teeth. His eyes, once warm with humanity, now gleamed with an otherworldly luminescence, betraying the emergence of his true nature.

Amidst the symphony of his shifting bones and the rustling leaves, Ruok's metamorphosis neared its conclusion. His body straightened, no longer human but a creature born of moonlight and shadow. He stood on powerful, muscular legs, his fur a deep, obsidian black that absorbed the moon's glow, giving him an almost ethereal aura. Each breath he took seemed to ripple with latent power, the embodiment of primal strength.

Suddenly Alex screamed and fell to the ground. Marcus and Scarlette stopped in their tracks in shock. When Alex stood up, he had an evil leer on his face and his features began to transform. His evil alter ego had begun to manifest. He threw back his head and laughed out loud.

"Well, hello, boys and girls." Lexa said with a sneer on his lips. "I hope I haven't missed much of this party."

"The party's just beginning, my young friend." Ruok walked up to Lexa, the darkness that was following the wolf man now formed a veil around him.

"So Ruok, you're not in danger anymore, I see." Lexa smiled at the wolf man.

"From this darkness of my own making?" Ruok laughed. "Not in the least."

"You've been lying to us all this while." Marcus pointed his D-Blaster at Ruok.

"Oh, that little gun won't even tickle me." Ruok stuck his long tongue out at Marcus.

"You're not from this dimension." Scarlette gnashed her teeth. "We're not falling for your bluff. Fry him, Marcus."

The blobs of darkness around Ruok intercepted and absorbed the crystals fired from the D-Blasters, and Lexa joined Ruok in a fit of laughter.

"Who are you and what do you want with Alex?" Scarlette asked the wolf man as she lowered her weapon.

"Tell us the truth, and not any of the lies you said earlier." Marcus fired one more blast before lowering his gun.

"Oh, my name truly is Ruok and I am running from the Dictator for real." Ruok smiled at them.

"But he's chasing me because he wants to punish me for trying to steal the sceptre which opened the Forbidden Dimension."

"Why are you doing this?" Scarlette demanded. "Why are you releasing the horrors from this forbidden place?"

"Why?" Ruok bared his sharp fangs. "Why you ask, dear girl?

To rule all the dimensions of course, and with a growing superpower like Lexa by my side,

I will be invincible."

"So, it was your evil that manipulated Alex into releasing his dark side and becoming Lexa." Marcus said with rage. "You're going to burn in hell for this."

"Hell is one of the dimensions I intend to rule over too," Ruok laughed out loud.

"And I'll be generous and offer you a chance to join me, since you were such good friends to Alex."

"What? Never!" Scarlette and Marcus yelled as one.

"Come, come, now children." Ruok grinned wide. "Be nice, there isn't anything else you can do otherwise."

"W-ell." Dippy the D-Phone sneered suddenly. "They did exactly that by stalling you long enough for me to do this."

The D-Phone flew out of a very startled Lexa's hand and burst out a bright flash of light. The darkness around Ruok dissipated and a bright portal opened up before them. A figure in full military uniform, mask and dark shades appeared. Behind the figure stood six others, tall and broad-shouldered men, in similar uniform.

The D-Phone flew out of a very startled Lexa's hand and burst out a bright flash of light.

The darkness around Ruok dissipated and a bright portal opened up before them. A giant figure in full golden military armour complete with a galea helmet and glowing sparkling eyes appeared.

Behind the figure stood six others, tall and broad-shouldered men, in similar uniform.

"Vezan." Ruok said in a small, yet fearful voice.

"You can't run anymore," Vezan the Dictator said in a voice that sounded like thunder... "Surrender, and your punishment may be lighter."

"I prefer no punishment at all," Ruok grinned and spread out his arms.

Out of thin air, a dozen Possessor Virus materialised and surrounded Ruok, then disappeared from sight along with him.

"He's gone" Scarlette said open mouthed.

"Not too far." Dictator Vezan said calmly. "He's invisible and hiding within the perimeter. I'll find him soon."

"Oh, look." Marcus pointed at Alex lying on the ground. "Alex is back."

"Uhhh... what happened?" Alex sat up and looked around groggily.

Alex's groggy voice broke through the tension, a welcome reminder of their shared humanity.

Scarlette let out a breath she didn't realise she was holding. "Alex, you're back."

Marcus extended a hand to help Alex up. "You had a bit of a rough time there, buddy."

Alex accepted Marcus's hand with a grateful smile, slowly standing up. "Rough is an understatement. But I can feel it, whatever darkness was inside me, it's gone."

Scarlette nodded, her eyes softening with relief. "It's over now. We're here for you."

The group gathered in a huddle, their emotions a mix of exhaustion and gratitude. The mall's surroundings seemed to echo their relief, the usual hustle and bustle of shoppers resuming as if nothing had happened.

Dictator Vezan approached them, his expression stoic yet revealing traces of curiosity. "It seems that you've managed to thwart Ruok's plans. For that, you have my thanks."

Alex's gaze met Vezan's, his voice holding a tinge of determination. "We're not out of the woods yet. Ruok may be gone, but there are still mysteries left to unravel."

Vezan's lips curved into a rare semblance of a smile. "Indeed, there's much left to discover. The dimensions hold more secrets than we can imagine."

As the group pondered the uncertainties ahead, Dippy's voice chimed in. "May I suggest a course of action? We should regroup and gather information. The Forbidden Dimension and Ruok's involvement might be just the tip of the iceberg."

Alex nodded in agreement. "Dippy's right. We need to prepare ourselves, understand the extent of the danger, and be ready for whatever challenges lie ahead."

Scarlette looked at Alex with unwavering determination. "We've faced the unknown before, and we've come out stronger. With our teamwork and resolve, we can overcome whatever comes our way."

Marcus cracked a small smile. "I can't believe I'm saying this, but she's right. Let's focus on gathering knowledge, arming ourselves with information that can give us an upper hand."

Vezan's gaze shifted between them, a sense of acknowledgment in his eyes. "You possess a remarkable strength, one that can't be underestimated. Your willingness to stand against chaos is commendable."

With Dippy's guidance, they delved deeper into the mysteries of the Forbidden Dimension, piecing together fragmented information and deciphering ancient texts that hinted at the realm's true nature.

The next day, their research led them to an old library nestled in a forgotten part of the city. Dust-covered shelves sagged under the weight of ancient tomes, and the scent of old paper and forgotten knowledge hung in the air. In the dim light, they pored over pages filled with accounts of otherworldly creatures, rifts between dimensions, and the power struggles that had shaped their existence.

"The Forbidden Dimension," Marcus mused, his finger tracing the words on a yellowed page. "It's like a nexus of unimaginable energies. No wonder it's considered off-limits."

Scarlette nodded, her eyes alight with fascination. "And it seems Ruok's actions weren't just about power. He was trying to exploit the dimension's potential for his own gains."

Alex leaned in, his brows furrowing in concentration. "But what about Lexa? How did that darkness take over me?"

As they exchanged theories and insights, Dictator Vezan's figure materialised at the library's entrance. "I've been monitoring your progress. It seems you're on the right track."

Their attention turned to Vezan, a mix of wariness and curiosity in their gazes. "What do you know about the Forbidden Dimension, Vezan?" Alex asked, his voice cautious.

Vezan's gaze held a depth of knowledge that sent shivers down their spines. "I've encountered its influence before. It's a realm that defies the laws of our dimensions, a place where the boundaries between light and darkness blur."

"Why was it forbidden in the first place?" Scarlette inquired, her curiosity piqued.

Vezan's expression darkened. "Because the Forbidden Dimension harbours not just power, but unspeakable horrors. Those creatures Ruok released were merely the beginning."

As the weight of his words settled in, a newfound determination filled the room. "We can't let those horrors spread," Marcus declared, his voice resolute.

Vezan nodded in agreement. "I'm prepared to offer my assistance, limited though it may be. We need to contain the breach, prevent these creatures from causing further chaos."

With the unlikely alliance forming, the group spent days refining their plan. They forged weapons capable of combating the unearthly creatures, researched rituals to seal the rifts, and honed their combat skills to face the unknown dangers that lay ahead.

the trio found themselves back at Trafalgar Square. The same place where their journey to confront Ruok had begun. The memories were bittersweet; a reminder of the challenges they had overcome.

"Seems like a lifetime ago," Marcus mused, his gaze fixed on the fountain's sparkling waters.

Alex nodded, a wistful smile on his lips. "We've come a long way since then."

Scarlette's eyes held a mixture of nostalgia and determination. "And there's still more to come. Our dimensions are safer, but the unknown will always be a part of our lives."

As they lingered in the square, a familiar figure approached. Dictator Vezan's presence was a testament to the enduring connections forged in the midst of chaos.

"An unexpected reunion," Vezan remarked, his gaze steady. "Your resilience has left an impression."

The group shared a knowing look, a silent acknowledgment of the bond they had formed. "We wouldn't have succeeded without your assistance," Alex said, gratitude evident in his voice.

Vezan's lips curved into a rare smile. "Our dimensions may be separate, but our fates remain intertwined. We must stay vigilant, for the threads of chaos are always ready to unravel."

Their conversation was interrupted by a familiar electronic voice. "Excuse me, everyone. I have some news."

Dippy's holographic form materialised, its screen displaying a map with blinking markers. "Unusual disturbances are being reported across various dimensions. It seems the effects of the Forbidden Dimension's breach still linger."

Scarlette's brow furrowed. "We thought we had sealed the rifts."

Dippy nodded. "You did, but there are residual energies that continue to cause disruptions. It's not as severe as before, but it's a reminder that the dimensions are connected in ways we can't fully comprehend."

Alex's gaze hardened, his determination reignited. "Then we're not done yet. We'll investigate these disturbances and put an end to whatever remnants of chaos remain."

Marcus clenched his fists, his resolve matching Alex's. "Our dimensions deserve peace. We'll face whatever challenges arise together."

Scarlette's voice held a mix of contemplation and determination. "We've faced darkness, conquered our fears, and emerged stronger."

Marcus nodded, his gaze fixed on the city lights below. "And the threads that tie our dimensions together are becoming clearer. It's as if the boundaries are fading."

Alex's thoughts mirrored his companions'. "We've come so far, but there's still much we don't understand. The Forbidden Dimension was just the beginning."

As they stood in silence, their senses were heightened by a ripple of energy that surged through the air. A dimensional rift shimmered into existence before them, a gateway to a world that seemed both familiar and foreign.

Vezan's voice carried on the wind. "It seems our destinies are intertwined once again."

The Dictator materialised before them, his presence a reminder of the uncharted path they walked. "The threads of chaos may have waned, but the fabric of our dimensions is changing."

Scarlette's gaze met Vezan's, curiosity in her eyes. "What do you mean?"

Vezan's gaze held a mixture of wisdom and gravitas. "The remnants of chaos have triggered an awakening. The dimensions are evolving, and with that comes both challenges and opportunities."

CHAPTER ELEVEN

"UNLEASHED SHADOWS: CITY IN CHAOS"

"Where is he now?" Alex asked. "And how can we stop him?"

"He's hiding somewhere." Vezan replied. "But I can find him... and so can you with your D-Phone."

"Okay." Alex nodded and held the D-Phone out before him. "Let's find him."

"You three go East and we'll go West." The Dictator said and marched away with his half dozen men.

"Alright then." Alex whispered to his friends. "Let's go, I think I found him. And let's not tell this dictator anything now. I don't trust him yet."

"I was thinking the same thing." Scarlette nodded. "Which way do you think Ruok went?"

"This way..." Alex pointed further eastward. "There, right under the Trafalgar Square Lion."

"Is he really there?" Marcus asked. "I don't see anything."

"The dictator said he could become invisible." Scarlette replied. "Be careful, Alex."

"I'm ready for him." Alex held the D-Phone out before him. "I know just the thing to use against..."

"Oh, look." Marcus pointed as the three of them stepped into the square. "Someone's there."

As they turned to look, it was Lucas and his gang, who had carved out a reputation for themselves as troublemakers in the area, had been keeping a close watch on the developments in the criminal underworld. They hoped to gain some insights into the success of the operation targeting the elusive "Sceptre," a prized artefact that many had sought for years.

As the news of the unsuccessful capture of the Sceptre spread through whispers in the shadows, Lucas's frustration simmered. His gang had been hoping for a significant power shift, a chance to establish themselves more firmly in the hierarchy of The Hood. The news shattered their dreams and ignited a dangerous spark within them.

In the heart of this turmoil, Lucas eyed Alex and his friends with an unsettling blend of jealousy and resentment. Breezy, one of Lucas's closest allies, seemed particularly agitated. Her emotions danced on a tightrope between her loyalty to Lucas and her deeper feelings for Alex. She had mastered the art of feigning animosity towards Alex, but cracks in her facade were beginning to show. In the midst of chaos, she found herself unable to entirely suppress the affection that had grown within her.

As tensions escalated, Breezy confronted Scarlette, attempting to mask her jealousy behind a veil of aggression. Her thinly veiled accusations revealed her inner turmoil, hinting at the complexity of emotions she had struggled to suppress. Scarlette's calm demeanour infuriated Breezy even more, a stark reminder of her own vulnerability.

Meanwhile, Lucas goaded Alex and his friends, attempting to provoke a fight that could elevate their standing in the eyes of the underground. But Alex's group, fuelled by a sense of camaraderie and an understanding of the bigger picture, refused to be drawn into a brawl. Their restraint only further infuriated Lucas and his gang, who felt their power slipping through their fingers.

Just when the situation seemed poised to erupt into violence, a horrifying presence emerged.

The very shadows seemed to come alive, writhing and twisting in unnatural ways. It was Ruok, an enigmatic force that held sway over the night and its terrors. Lucas and his gang, who had once projected an air of invincibility, were reduced to cowering in fear before the manifestations of Ruok's power.

The encounter with Ruok served as a harsh reminder of the true forces at play,

Lucas and his gang realised that forces more powerful than their own dwarfed the ambitions of The Hood.. In their retreat, fear etched into their faces, their bravado shattered and replaced with a chilling realisation of their insignificance.

And in the midst of it all, Breezy found herself at a crossroads, torn between her loyalty to Lucas, her feelings for Alex, and the unfolding darkness that threatened to consume them all.

The Trafalgar Square lion, an iconic symbol of the city, stood transformed. Its stony form had grown even larger, a colossal monstrosity that cast a shadow over the entire city. Its once lifeless eyes now burned with malevolent red light, a fiery glare that sent chills down the spines of all who beheld it.

Central London was plunged into chaos. The iconic landmarks and historic streets became a battleground of fear as the possessed lion roared, its deafening cry echoing through the city streets. The army and police forces had mobilised, armed with heavy weaponry that erupted in bursts of fire and thunder. But their efforts were in vain; bullets ricocheted off the lion's stone exterior, and the red glow in its eyes only intensified.

Panic spread like wildfire as citizens ran for cover, their cries joining the cacophony of chaos. Sirens wailed, and the blaring lights of emergency vehicles painted the streets with a surreal glow.

The military's best attempts to halt the rampage of the lion proved futile, and the heart of London seemed to be held captive by an unstoppable force.

Amidst the turmoil, Scarlette and Marcus shared a moment of genuine fear. The magnitude of the situation was beyond anything they had ever encountered. The once-stationary lion was now a living nightmare, an embodiment of ancient power that had been unleashed upon the city.

Even Alex, who had faced danger countless times, couldn't suppress the trepidation that flickered in his eyes.

Alex's voice cut through the fear, a beacon of determination amidst the chaos. "We've come too far to give up now," he reminded them, his gaze steady. "We've faced challenges before, and we'll face this one together."

As if to punctuate his words, the ground shuddered beneath their feet, and the lion unleashed a roar that shook the very foundations of the city. Its thunderous reverberations seemed to awaken the collective spirit of defiance within the group. Scarlette, Marcus, and Alex exchanged glances of unwavering resolve, their fear transformed into a united front against the encroaching darkness.

They joined forces with the military and police, marshalling their courage against the supernatural threat. The scene became a desperate battlefield, with D-Blasters firing powerful beams at the colossal lion. But the creature's form remained unscathed, and its red eyes blazed with unholy fury.

Scarlette and Marcus fought valiantly, but their efforts came at a great cost. The lion's ferocity was unmatched, and they were seriously injured in the process. The battle raged on, leaving destruction in its wake.

Amidst the chaos, a new glimmer of hope emerged. Vezan returned, his aura radiating ancient magic and determination. He revealed himself to be a force of good, seeking to put an end to Ruok's malevolent reign confirming Alex' theory. Mr. Ransford, Dippy, and their friends stood by his side, united in their purpose.

With the lion's relentless pursuit, the group made a daring escape on a London bus, the massive creature hot on their heels. The streets blurred by as they sped through the city, the lion's thunderous footsteps reverberating in their ears. The chase was a heart-pounding nightmare, the looming threat of destruction always close behind.

In a climactic moment, Alex finally seized the magic sceptre. Its power surged through him, a surge of energy that resonated with his very soul.

He turned to face the charging lion, channelling the sceptre's magic into a brilliant display of radiant energy. The air crackled with power as a blinding beam of light shot forth, colliding with the lion in a titanic clash of forces.

The battle that followed was intense and fierce. The lion's monstrous might clashed with the combined efforts of the group, the very city itself becoming a battlefield of magic and stone. Each strike reverberated with the weight of their struggle.

Then, with a final surge of power, the lion's form shattered, dispersing like dust in the wind. The red glow in its eyes faded and Ruok screamed "Noooooooooooo!" as the sceptre opened a portal into the forbidden dimension that Ruok got sucked into where it's horrors awaited him. The city fell silent as the night reclaimed its peace.

Exhausted but triumphant, the group gathered amidst the wreckage. Scarlette and Marcus received medical attention, their injuries a testament to the cost of their bravery. As dawn broke over the city, its streets scarred but resilient, the group stood together, knowing that their unity and courage had triumphed over the darkest of forces.

With the lion defeated, a hushed calm settled over the city, broken only by the distant sounds of sirens and the soft hum of emergency lights.

The residents of London, who had hidden in fear, cautiously emerged from their shelters, their eyes wide with awe and trepidation. The shattered remains of the once-mighty lion lay scattered across Trafalgar Square, a stark reminder of the extraordinary battle that had unfolded in their midst.

The group of friends stood together amidst the wreckage, their faces marked with sweat, dirt, and the undeniable signs of a hard-fought victory. The camaraderie that had grown between them was stronger than ever, forged through adversity and shared purpose. They surveyed the horizon, where the sun was beginning to rise, casting hues of orange and pink across the sky.

Over the following days, London began the process of recovery. Clean-up crews worked tirelessly to clear the debris, and a sense of unity seemed to pervade the air. Messages of gratitude poured in from citizens who had witnessed the group's heroic efforts, and media outlets hailed them as the "Defenders of London," their story spreading far and wide.

Yet, victory came at a cost. Scarlette and Marcus faced a challenging road to recovery, their injuries a stark reminder of the danger they had faced. However, their determination to protect their city remained unwavering, and the bonds they had formed with their friends only grew stronger in the face of adversity.

Life in London gradually returned to a semblance of normalcy. The shattered remnants of the lion were removed from Trafalgar Square, and plans for its restoration began to take shape. The group's adventures had left an indelible mark on the city, a testament to the resilience of its inhabitants and the unwavering spirit of unity.

During their moments of respite, the group often found themselves gathered in the park, where the once-menacing lion had stood. As they looked upon the spot where the battle had taken place, a shared understanding passed between them. They were more than friends; they were a family forged through shared trials and triumphs.

CHAPTER TWELVE

RETURN OF THE SCEPTRE

After the intense battles and the victory over Ruok's dark schemes, Alex and his friends returned to Esmeira with the Ancient Sacred Sceptre in hand.

The portal shimmered before them, offering a passage back to the world beyond.

As they stepped through the portal, they found themselves once again in the mystical land of Esmeira. The vibrant colours, the swirling magic in the air, and the ethereal landscapes were a welcome sight. They were greeted by familiar faces – the majestic creatures, the curious beings, and the enchanting scenery they had come to know during their time there.

Walking through the lush meadows, they were met by a procession of Esmeiran beings, led by none other than Vesta herself.

Her presence radiated warmth and power, and her eyes held a mix of gratitude and pride as she looked upon the group of heroes who had saved both their worlds.

"Alex Knight, Scarlette, Marcus, and all of you," Vesta's voice echoed like a gentle breeze. "You have shown remarkable bravery and determination. Esmeira and your world owe you a debt of gratitude."

Scarlette blushed, her eyes sparkling with a mixture of awe and humility. "We were just doing what needed to be done."

Marcus nodded in agreement. "Yeah, and we had some pretty amazing help along the way."

Vesta's gaze lingered on Alex, her eyes filled with a sense of admiration.

"You, Alex Knight, have proven yourself to be a true hero of both dimensions. You've embraced your destiny with courage and heart."

Alex's blushed as he rubbed the back of his neck. "I couldn't have done it without my friends."

Vesta raised her hand, and a gentle breeze enveloped them. When it subsided, each of Alex's friends held a token of appreciation a symbol of their courage and unity.

"These tokens will forever remind you of the bond you share and the extraordinary journey you've undertaken."

As the tokens gleamed in their hands, Vesta's expression turned more serious. "But remember, the balance between our worlds is delicate. The threat may be gone for now, but darkness can always find its way back. Stay vigilant and united, for your actions have consequences that ripple through the dimensions."

With a nod, Alex, Scarlette, and Marcus promised to heed her words.

In the days that followed, they were celebrated as heroes throughout Esmeira. Festivals were held in their honour, and the people of this mystical land rejoiced in the victory over the darkness that had threatened to engulf their world.

As they basked in the celebrations, Alex's gaze wandered across the vibrant crowd. Suddenly, his heart skipped a beat as he spotted a familiar face among the revellers. It was Lily, the friend he had first encountered when he arrived in Esmeira. She had played a pivotal role in guiding him through this enchanting world during his initial bewildering days.

Overwhelmed with joy, Alex excused himself from the crowd and rushed over to her. Lyra turned, her eyes widening in pleasant surprise as she recognised him. "Alex? Is that really you?"

He grinned from ear to ear, pulling her into a tight hug. "Lyra, it's me! I can't believe you're here!"

Lyra laughed, her voice tinkling like wind chimes. "I heard about the heroes who saved Esmeira, you've become a legend."

Alex chuckled, feeling a sense of completeness in this reunion.

"You were the one who showed me the ropes here, Lyra. I couldn't have done any of this without you."

As the festivities continued, Alex and Lyra shared stories of their adventures since they had last seen each other. Their connection, which had been formed in the midst of uncertainty, had grown stronger through their shared experiences.

When the time came for Alex and his friends to depart from Esmeira, he promised Lyra that he would return someday. Their farewells were heartfelt, and as they stepped through the portal once again, Alex carried with him not only the gratitude of Esmeira but also the renewed friendship that had blossomed in the midst of their extraordinary journey.

Back in London, the aftermath of the battle against Ruok left its mark on both the physical landscape and the lives of its citizens. The city's resilience, however, was a testament to its enduring spirit. As rebuilding efforts continued, a sense of unity and cooperation permeated the air, strengthening the bonds between neighbours and strangers alike.

In the wake of the battle, something extraordinary began to happen. Those who had been afflicted by the vampire virus, their minds clouded by Ruok's malevolent influence, slowly started to regain control over their thoughts and actions. It was as if a fog was lifting from their minds, allowing them to remember their true selves.

Alex and his friends, now seen as heroes, worked tirelessly to aid those affected by the virus. They collaborated with scientists, doctors, and researchers to develop a cure that would fully restore the afflicted individuals to their original states. It was a daunting challenge, but their determination was unyielding.

With the help of Vezan's extensive knowledge of magic, Dippy and Mr. Ransford's, a breakthrough was achieved. The combined efforts of both worlds yielded a cure that effectively eliminated the vampire virus and erased the influence of Ruok. The process was not without its difficulties; the cure required a delicate balance of magic and science, and its successful application was a testament to the power of collaboration.

As the cure spread through London, those who had once been under Ruok's control experienced a moment of awakening. The confusion and darkness that had clouded their minds dissipated, replaced by a flood of memories and emotions. People who had been friends, family, and loved ones were reunited in tearful embraces, their bonds renewed and strengthened by their shared struggle.

One of the most touching reunions was that of Paul, who had been among the possessed. As the effects of the cure took hold, his eyes regained their clarity, and the deep connection he felt for Alex became evident.

The defeat of Ruok marked a turning point not only for London but also for the entire supernatural realm.

The balance between light and darkness had been restored, and the lessons learned from the ordeal were etched into the collective memory. The people of both worlds recognised the importance of unity, courage, and compassion in the face of adversity.

With the cure's success, hope and relief spread like wildfire throughout London. The city's streets buzzed with life once more, as those who had been affected by the vampire virus reintegrated into society. Reunions between families, friends, and loved ones filled the air with tears of joy and laughter.

Breezy's transformation from the influence of Her feelings for Alex, once suppressed, blossomed into a deep and genuine connection. As she navigated her emotions, Breezy found herself becoming an advocate for unity and understanding, sharing her own experiences to inspire others to embrace change and growth.

As life settled into a new normal, Alex, Scarlette, Marcus, and their friends continued to be recognised as heroes both in London and Esmeira. The bond they had forged through their trials remained unbreakable, and their shared memories served as a reminder of the strength that could be found in unity.

The relationship between the two worlds deepened as well. Cultural exchanges, trade, and cooperation became the norm, as the boundaries that once separated London and Esmeira began to blur. The heroes' legacy extended beyond their individual acts of bravery, shaping a future where understanding and collaboration triumphed over fear and isolation.

In a quiet moment, Alex found himself standing at the edge of Trafalgar Square, gazing at the statue that had once been the source of chaos. Now restored, the lion stood as a symbol of the city's resilience. Scarlette joined him, her presence a comforting reminder of the journey they had shared.

"Can you believe how far we've come?" Alex mused, his eyes fixed on the lion.

Scarlette smiled and kissed Alex on the cheek leaving him temporarily blushing in which Marcus laughed. Her gaze contemplative. "It's incredible, isn't it? We faced the darkest of forces and emerged stronger because of it."

"And it's all thanks to our unity," Alex added, glancing at her. "I couldn't have asked for better friends to stand by my side."

Scarlette's fingers found his, their touch a testament to the unspoken bond between them. "We're not just friends, Alex. We're a family, brought together by circumstances but bound by choice."

As the sun set on London, casting a warm and golden glow over the city, Alex and Scarlette shared a moment of quiet understanding. Their journey had been one of growth, not just as individuals, but as a group.

The challenges they had faced had transformed them into heroes who inspired change and hope.

CHAPTER THIRTEEN

"RESILIENT HEARTS: A JOURNEY OF REDEMPTION AND TRANSFORMATION"

The aftermath of the intense battle against the toxic vampires left a sense of both relief and reflection in the air.

Mr. Paul, Alex's stepdad felt a sense of humility he hadn't experienced in years, an acknowledgement that he was but one small part of a much larger tapestry. The battles had not only tested his strength but also his convictions, revealing the limits of his understanding and the fallibility of his judgements.

As he contemplated the events of the past days, he couldn't help but recall the pivotal moment during the battle when Alex had saved his life. The memory played like a vivid scene in his mind the vampire's lethal strike halted by a swift, decisive movement, the glint of the silver blade, and the sound of shattering bones as the creature crumbled to dust. In that moment, his stepson had become his saviour, his protector.

His footsteps were laden with a mixture of awe and humility. There was a newfound respect in his eyes, a respect born from acknowledging the strength and courage his stepson had displayed.

The realisation struck him like a bolt of lightning his stepson was no longer the struggling student he had once dismissed; he was a force to be reckoned with, a beacon of hope in a world teetering on the edge of darkness.

"I misjudged you, Alex," he admitted, his voice carrying a touch of regret and sincerity. "I didn't realise the kind of person you've become. You're not just a kid anymore – you're a hero."

Alex's heart swelled at the weight of those words. The validation he had longed for, the recognition of his worth that had eluded him, was finally being offered in a way he had never imagined. Tears welled in his eyes, a mixture of relief, validation, and gratitude. He had fought not only to save the city but also to prove his worth to himself and those who had doubted him.

The emotional release he had been suppressing throughout the ordeal finally found an outlet. The walls he had built around his vulnerability crumbled in the face of his stepdad's acknowledgement. In that moment, he realised that his stepdad's transformation was as significant as his own – a transformation from scepticism to belief, from detachment to connection.

Their surroundings seemed to fade into the background as the two of them shared a moment of profound connection. The debris-strewn landscape became a backdrop to their reconciliation, a symbol of the hurdles they had overcome individually and together. It wasn't just about defeating supernatural foes; it was about conquering the barriers within their own hearts.

From that point on, their relationship underwent a profound transformation.

While they still had their differences and occasional moments of tension, there was a newfound sense of empathy and mutual respect. Conversations that had once been strained were now marked by genuine interest and understanding. They listened to each other, truly heard each other's perspectives, and acknowledged each other's growth.

In the weeks that followed, as London slowly reclaimed its rhythm and the scars of battle were gradually erased, Alex and his friends found solace in the knowledge that their struggles had not only saved their world but had also initiated positive change in their lives. The once ordinary teenagers had been forged into a tight-knit group, bound not only by shared experiences but by an unbreakable bond of friendship.

As the city's wounds healed, Alex's stepdad actively supported his stepson's aspirations. He became a vocal advocate for Alex's endeavours, utilising his influence to help the young hero make a tangible impact on their community. The support he provided wasn't just symbolic; it was a testament to the transformation that had occurred within both of them.

The news of their victory spread far and wide, reaching the ears of citizens and officials alike. Alex and his friends were lauded as heroes, celebrated for their bravery and selflessness. The accolades were appreciated, but it was the personal growth they had achieved that truly mattered to them. They had faced their fears, conquered their doubts, and emerged stronger than they had ever thought possible.

In the quiet moments between battles and celebrations, Alex took the time to reflect on his journey.

The battles had taught him that heroism wasn't just about physical strength; it was about resilience, compassion, and the willingness to stand up for what was right. He had proven not only to others but also to himself that he was capable of making a difference, no matter how insurmountable the odds.

As for his stepdad, he found himself inspired by the transformation he had witnessed in his stepson. He had learned that strength could manifest in various forms, and that humility and the willingness to learn from one's mistakes were essential for personal growth. The battles against the toxic vampires had not only saved their city but had also salvaged a fractured relationship, turning it into something stronger and more meaningful.

And so, as the sun set on the city, casting vibrant hues across the sky, a sense of hope and renewal lingered in the air. The battles were over, but their impact was far-reaching.

The story of Alex and his stepdad was a testament to the power of change, the resilience of the human spirit, and the potential for transformation that exists within every individual.

The once-devastated streets were now bustling with renewed activity, a testament to the city's resilience and the unwavering spirit of its people.

In the midst of the rebuilding process, Alex's stepdad remained a steady presence in his life.

The change in their relationship was palpable to those around them. Friends and family noticed the way they interacted – the shared glances, the genuine conversations, and the mutual respect that had replaced the tension of the past. It was as though a bridge had been built, a bridge constructed from the debris of their old misunderstandings.

One sunny afternoon, as they stood on a balcony overlooking the city's progress, Alex and his stepdad shared a rare moment of introspection. The sounds of construction and bustling streets provided a backdrop to their conversation.

"You know, I used to think that being strong meant never showing weakness," Alex's stepdad began, his voice tinged with a hint of vulnerability. "But you showed me that strength comes from acknowledging our weaknesses and facing them head-on."

Alex turned to him, a smile playing at the corners of his lips. "It's not about being invulnerable; it's about being resilient. And I learned that from you too. You faced your own doubts and changed your perspective. That takes a different kind of strength."

His stepdad nodded, his gaze fixed on the horizon. "I used to believe that success was measured by power and authority. But watching you and your friends fight for what's right made me realise that true success lies in making a positive impact on the world around us."

As they spoke, it was as though their words were building a bridge of understanding between them, spanning the gap that had once seemed insurmountable. Their shared experiences had forged a connection that couldn't be broken, a connection rooted in their growth and transformation.

Months passed, and the city continued to mend. The scars of battle faded, replaced by a newfound appreciation for the ordinary moments that made up daily life. Alex and his friends resumed their studies, their friendships deepening as they navigated the challenges of both school and heroism.

One evening, Alex sat in his room, poring over a book on history. His stepdad entered, carrying a tray of tea. They exchanged a knowing smile as his stepdad set the tray down on the table beside him.

"Tea break?" Alex asked, raising an eyebrow.

"Tea break," his stepdad confirmed with a chuckle. They settled into a comfortable silence, the only sound the gentle rustling of pages and the clinking of tea cups.

"You know," Alex began after a moment, "I never thought I'd see the day when we'd share moments like these."

His stepdad took a sip of his tea, considering his words. "Life has a way of surprising us. And I'm grateful for this chance to connect with you."

Their conversations had shifted from strained to sincere, from obligatory to authentic. Their shared experiences had shattered the barriers that had once divided them, allowing them to see each other as individuals with their own dreams, fears, and aspirations.

On weekend, Alex's stepdad suggested they take a walk in the park. It was a simple gesture, but it held a profound meaning a symbol of their journey towards understanding and acceptance. As they strolled along the tree-lined paths, they talked about everything from their favourite books to their aspirations for the future.

"I used to think that being a father meant having all the answers," his stepdad admitted with a wistful smile. "But the truth is, we're all figuring things out as we go along."

"Exactly," Alex agreed. "We're all on this journey, trying to make sense of the world and our place in it."

As the conversation flowed, Alex's stepdad stopped by a small pond. They watched as ripples formed on the water's surface, each one a reflection of the changes they had undergone.

As they walked back home, side by side, there was a sense of harmony in their steps – a harmony born from the unity they had found amidst chaos, from the bond they had forged through trials and triumphs. The city around them was rebuilding, growing stronger from the challenges it had faced. And within their hearts, a similar transformation had taken place, leaving them both forever changed.

The story of Alex and his stepdad was a testament to the fact that growth could emerge from the unlikeliest of places, that understanding could blossom from the seeds of adversity. It was a story of redemption, of second chances, and of the enduring power of love and connection. And as their journey continued, they knew that the battles they had faced had not only saved their city but had also set them on a path towards a future filled with hope, possibility, and the unwavering belief in the strength of the human spirit.

The days turned into weeks, and the weeks into months, as the city continued its healing process. The wounds of the battles were now mostly hidden beneath the layers of progress and growth. New buildings rose from the ashes, parks were restored, and the bustling sounds of everyday life returned with a renewed energy.

Alex and his friends had become local legends, their bravery and selflessness echoing through the city's streets. They were no longer just ordinary teenagers they were beacons of hope, symbols of what individuals could achieve when they came together for a common cause.

One evening, as they sat in the living room of their apartment, Alex's stepdad broached a subject that had once been a source of contention between them – Alex's dreams and aspirations.

"You know, Alex," he began, "after everything we've been through, I've come to realise that I should have supported your dreams from the start."

Alex looked up, surprised by the admission. "It's never too late to make amends, and I want to do whatever I can to help you achieve your goals."

Alex felt a mixture of gratitude and validation wash over him. His stepdad's change of heart was proof that people could grow, learn, and change their perspectives. The support he had yearned for was now being extended to him in ways he had never thought possible.

"Thank you," Alex said, his voice filled with sincerity. "It means a lot to me."

As the months passed, Alex's stepdad kept his promise, offering guidance and resources to help Alex pursue his passions. Together, they worked on projects that combined their unique strengths – Alex's creativity and his stepdad's business acumen. The partnership was a testament to their newfound understanding and the power of collaboration.

The city had recovered, but it wasn't the same city it had been before. It was stronger, more united, and more resilient. The battles against the toxic vampires had left an indelible mark on its inhabitants, a reminder of what could be achieved when people came together to protect what they cherished most.

as Alex and his friends gathered in a park, reminiscing about their experiences, a reporter approached them. The city had organised a celebration to honour their bravery and dedication. Amidst cheers and applause, Alex's stepdad stood by his side, a proud smile on his face.

Addressing the crowd, Alex spoke from the heart. "Our city faced a challenge that seemed insurmountable, but we learned that even in the darkest of times, there is light. We found that strength doesn't just come from physical power, but from unity, compassion, and the belief that we can make a difference."

The crowd erupted in cheers, their gratitude and admiration evident in their applause. But it was the presence of Alex's stepdad, standing by his side, that spoke volumes about the journey they had undertaken.

As the event concluded and the sun set on the horizon, painting the sky with shades of orange and pink, Alex and his stepdad found themselves once again on a balcony overlooking the city. The view was a testament to their shared journey – a city that had weathered storms, overcome challenges, and emerged stronger than ever.

"You've come a long way, Alex," his stepdad said, his voice filled with pride. "I've come a long way too."

Alex smiled, his heart full of gratitude. "We all have. And I wouldn't have it any other way."

Their shared experiences had transformed their relationship from one of conflict to one of connection. They had discovered that heroes could emerge from the unlikeliest of places – not just in the battles fought on the streets, but in the battles fought within the human heart.

As they looked out over the city, it was clear that their journey was far from over. New challenges would arise, new battles would be fought, but they faced the future with a sense of unity and determination that had been born from their past experiences.

Time flowed like a river, carrying with it the memories and lessons of the past. The seasons changed, each bringing its own colours and challenges to the city. Through it all, Alex and his stepdad continued to evolve, individually and together.

Alex's pursuits began to bear fruit. The projects he had embarked upon with his stepdad's support started to gain traction. Their collaborations were met with success, not just financially, but in the positive impact they had on the community. Their joint efforts to create opportunities for young artists, support local businesses, and contribute to various charitable causes became a cornerstone of their relationship.

as the city's skyline shimmered with the hues of a setting sun, Alex and his stepdad sat on the same balcony that had witnessed their journey of transformation. The familiar backdrop had become a canvas on which they painted their hopes and dreams.

"You've accomplished so much, Alex," his stepdad remarked, a genuine pride in his voice. "I'm proud to have been a part of this journey with you."

Alex leaned back, taking in the city's panorama. "And I'm grateful for your support, for believing in me when I needed it the most."

"You know," his stepdad began, his voice soft, "these battles taught us that heroism isn't just about victory. It's about the sacrifices we make for the greater good."

Alex nodded in agreement. "It's about facing our fears and standing up for what's right, even when the odds are against us."

As they stood there, surrounded by the hushed reverence of the memorial, their shared silence spoke volumes. The battles had shaped their lives, but they had also shaped their understanding of themselves and each other. The city's scars were now a testament to its resilience, just as the marks on their hearts were a testament to their growth.

Alex's stepdad became an advocate for unity and positive change within the city. His influence as a respected figure in the community allowed him to drive initiatives that fostered collaboration, support, and growth. The man who had once been defined by his scepticism was now defined by his willingness to believe in the potential of people and the power of transformation.

Alex's stepdad's journey of change was a source of inspiration not just for him, but for others as well.

His story became a beacon of hope for those who struggled with their own doubts and limitations, proving that change was possible and that every individual had the capacity to evolve.

It became a vibrant hub of creativity, innovation, and community engagement. The battles against the toxic vampires had left an indelible mark, not just on the physical landscape, but on the hearts of its inhabitants.

Alex and his stepdad found themselves back at the park that had been the epicentre of their journey. As they sat on a bench, looking out at the peaceful scene before them, Alex spoke, his words carrying the weight of gratitude.

"I used to think that heroes were only found in stories," he mused. "But I've come to realise that heroes are ordinary people who do extraordinary things, who face their fears and fight for what's right."

His stepdad nodded in agreement. "And I've learned that heroes can emerge from the unlikeliest of places, even from within ourselves."

Their journey had come full circle – from scepticism to acceptance, from conflict to understanding.

The battles they had fought had been the catalyst for their transformation, igniting a spark that had illuminated the path of growth and change.

As the sun began to dip below the horizon, casting a warm glow over the park, Alex and his stepdad shared a moment of quiet reflection. The battles were over, but their impact was far-reaching. The story of their shared struggles had evolved into one of mutual respect, shared goals, and a newfound appreciation for each other's strengths.

Alex's artistic endeavours flourished, his creations adorning the city's walls and galleries. His stepdad's business acumen and support played a crucial role in bringing his work to a wider audience. Their collaborations had not only fostered personal growth but had also contributed to the cultural richness of the city they both loved.

as Alex stood before a mural he had created in a bustling neighbourhood, he marvelled at the vibrant colours and intricate details that adorned the wall. It was a visual representation of his journey – a journey that had started with uncertainty and evolved into a vibrant tapestry of experiences and lessons.

His stepdad joined him, a smile tugging at the corners of his lips. "You've turned this city into a canvas, Alex. Your art speaks to people in ways words can't."

Alex nodded, his gaze fixed on the mural. "Art has a way of connecting us, of telling stories that transcend boundaries."

Their journey had indeed bridged boundaries, not just between individuals but within themselves. The battles against the toxic vampires had been the catalyst for their transformation, but it was their willingness to learn, to change, and to connect that had fuelled their growth.

As the years went by, Alex's stepdad-initiated community projects that aimed to empower the city's youth. He recognised that change started with the next generation, and he was determined to provide opportunities for them to discover their own potential. His efforts were a testament to the profound impact the battles had on his perspective.

as they walked through a newly revitalised neighbourhood, Alex's stepdad turned to him. "You know, Alex, I used to think that success was measured solely by accomplishments. But the battles we faced taught me that true success is about the positive influence we have on others."

Alex smiled, his stepdad's words resonating deeply. "The battles weren't just about defeating supernatural threats; they were about shaping the course of our lives and the lives of those around us."

As the city continued to thrive and evolve, Alex and his stepdad found themselves standing before the same memorial that had once marked the battleground. The names of the fallen were a reminder of the sacrifices made for the city's survival. The memorial was no longer a site of mourning; it was a site of remembrance and reverence.

"We owe it to them to continue pushing for positive change," Alex's stepdad said, his voice filled with determination.

Alex nodded, his gaze fixed on the memorial. "Their sacrifice was a testament to the strength of the human spirit, to the lengths we're willing to go to protect what matters."

As they stood there, a sense of gratitude enveloped them – gratitude for the battles they had faced, for the growth they had undergone, and for the unity they had discovered. Their individual journeys had converted into a shared narrative, a story that celebrated the potential for transformation in the face of adversity.

In the distance, the city's lights began to twinkle as night descended. The battles against the toxic vampires had left an indelible mark, not just on the physical landscape, but on the hearts of its inhabitants. The scars were a testament to the city's resilience, just as the marks on their hearts were a testament to their growth.

And so, as the stars emerged one by one in the velvety sky, Alex and his stepdad walked away from the memorial, their steps echoing with purpose.

CHAPTER FOURTEEN

"THE PRANK PORTAL: UNVEILING UNITY, CREATIVITY, AND LAUGHTER"

Their adventure in Esmeira had come to an end, but the memories and lessons they had gained would stay with them forever. They were heroes, not just in Esmeira, but in their world as well – united by friendship, bravery, and the unshakeable belief that even in the face of darkness, light would prevail.

As the summer holidays approached, Alex and his friends couldn't shake off the excitement of the entrepreneurial course they had taken in school. The lessons they had learned about creativity, innovation, and teamwork still buzzed in their minds, igniting a spark of potential they hadn't felt before. Their previous adventures had taught them the power of their unity, and now they were determined to channel that unity into a creative endeavour.

Their minds were buzzing with ideas, and one idea in particular caught fire: creating an online clothing store that would resonate with both kids and adults. Drawing inspiration from their diverse backgrounds and interests, they envisioned a collection that would not only reflect their personal styles but also cater to the unique tastes of their followers.

With determination and creativity, they divided into three teams, each with a unique theme. Alex led Team Grey Knight Wear, specialising in clothing that carried the symbol of a noble knight. Their designs spoke of honour, strength, and resilience, appealing to those who sought a touch of medieval flair in their modern wardrobe.

Marcus spearheaded Team 90s Nostalgia, reviving the vibrant and nostalgic style of the 1990s with their bold and colourful designs. From oversized denim jackets to neon windbreakers, their collection transported customers back in time, evoking memories of a bygone era and resonating with those who cherished pop culture's golden age.

Scarlette took charge of Team Scarlet Urban, designing urban wear in varying shades of red, all adorned with a captivating symbol of a scarlet bird. Her collection exuded confidence, with sleek street wear that captured attention and sparked conversations about empowerment and self-expression.

The online store launched with a bang, catching the attention of their followers and quickly gaining traction among fashion enthusiasts. Their merchandise flew off the digital shelves, and they found themselves running a thriving business that also reflected their individual personalities. The experience of managing their store taught them more than just entrepreneurship – it reinforced the importance of effective communication, customer service, and adaptability.

As the end of summer approached, the store had achieved unexpected success. The friends revelled in their accomplishment and the memories they had made, but they couldn't shake off the feeling that this was only the beginning of their journey. Their bond had grown stronger through shared creativity and the challenges of running a business together.

The next day, as they were packing up their merchandise to ship out, a mysterious email landed in their shared inbox. It contained a cryptic message, speaking of trouble in another dimension that needed their attention.

The message was written in a language that felt both ancient and alien, and its urgency was palpable even through the digital words.

The friends exchanged glances, their curiosity piqued. Is this a prank? Alex muttered, his eyebrows furrowed. Or was this some sort of elaborate marketing scheme? Marcus chimed in, scepticism tainting his voice. Scarlette, however, gazed at the screen with a mix of curiosity and excitement, her adventurous spirit ignited once again.

Curiosity got the better of them, and after much debate, they decided to investigate. The email contained coordinates and instructions on how to access the alternate dimension. It was an audacious decision, one that could lead them into the unknown, but they couldn't ignore the possibility that there might be something genuine and extraordinary awaiting them.

With a mixture of intrigue and apprehension, the friends embarked on the journey outlined in the mysterious email. They followed the coordinates to a remote location outside of town, where they found an odd-looking device placed on a pedestal. It had an otherworldly design, with glowing symbols etched into its surface.

As they approached the device, a sense of excitement and wonder filled the air. Scarlette's adventurous spirit burned even brighter, while Alex and Marcus exchanged uncertain glances. Could this truly be a portal to another dimension, or were they falling for an elaborate prank?

Scarlette, always the first to embrace the unknown, reached out and interacted with the device according to the instructions. There was a shimmer in the air, a distortion of reality, and suddenly, the world around them seemed to shift. Colours became more vibrant, and the landscape took on an otherworldly hue.

But before they could fully process what was happening, a burst of confetti erupted around them, and the air was filled with the sound of laughter. The scene before them transformed from a fantastical landscape to their own familiar surroundings, now adorned with streamers and balloons.

Out of the shadows stepped their classmates and friends, all wearing mischievous grins. It was then that the truth hit them – the email, the device, and the alternate dimension were all part of an elaborately orchestrated prank.

The laughter that erupted was a chorus of genuine amusement, and the relief that washed over Alex, Marcus, and Scarlette was palpable.

As they realised the extent of the prank, the friends couldn't help but join in the laughter. Scarlette playfully punched Alex's arm, and Marcus shook his head in mock disbelief. Their scepticism had turned out to be warranted, and yet, the unexpected twist filled them with a sense of camaraderie and shared humour.

Amidst the laughter, their friends explained how they had devised the plan to create the mysterious email and set up the whimsical portal-like contraption. It was all in good fun, a celebration of their success with the online store and a testament to the strength of their friendship.

Milton Keynes UK
Ingram Content Group UK Ltd.
UKHW020658091123
432260UK00018B/460